THE WOLF PACK

THE WOLF PACK

by Fritz Leiber

CHAPTER 1

Just inside the weatherdome Normsi stripped off his flying togs and hung them on the family rack. He noticed Allisoun's and her brother Willisoun's, his father's and mother's, and his own walking togs.

Outside it was chilly winter with a low red sun, but under the intangible hemisphere of the weatherdome the atoms were domesticated. Here were light, heat, life-giving radiation. The warm, moist air moved in gentle currents—a little kept leaking from the lee side of the dome, to condense into white vapor and whirl away.

Flowers bloomed, buds opened, grass pushed up. Here was perpetual spring.

Norm's world was like the weatherdome. He was a healthy, well-educated, uninjured young man, had an attractive job as a teletaction technician, looked forward to an early marriage with the girl he loved.

A world economy of abundance supplied him with conveniences, luxuries, and recreations almost beyond the dreams of earlier ages. There were even charming female psychiatrists to teach him sexual behavior.

A single government had ruled the world for two centuries. There had been no civil war for more than a hundred years.

The exploration of the nearer planets had brought to light no intelligent or dangerous non-intelligent enemies of mankind. Indeed, the opening up of Mars and Venus had proved rather anticlimactic, since their harsh environments prevented easy colonization and Earth's synthetics-based self-sufficiency took the urgency from the search for new sources of mineral and organic wealth. The new planets would serve chiefly as stations for cosmological research, until gradual scientific exploration of their life-patterns opened yet unseen vistas.

Nor was Norm's body the uneasy prey of disease germs and degenerative processes. He had far better than a 99 percent chance of escaping such dangers as long as he lived.

THE WOLF PACK

Yet, standing there in the garden beside the togs-rack, Norm did not look like that fortunate man. If his eyes had been closed, his face would have registered as young, fresh, healthy. But with them open, the fear of death infected every feature.

He delayed near the togs-rack, running his hand through his close-cropped hair, smoothing his pajama neckband, where a line of red, white, and blue recalled the necktie of ancient times.

With a sudden headshake, he started up the path toward the house. Halfway there his eye strayed to the grass. He pushed at a weed with the toe of his moccasin, remained staring at the tiny green world at his feet.

Even the vastest weatherdome has its outside, its region of storms and darkness and the unknown.

An ant struggled up one of the grassblades. Without thinking he set his foot on it, then drew back, wincing as though he had glimpsed something particularly unpleasant, and hurried on to the house. As the door opened, he readied his lips for a grin of relief.

But the grin never came. He stopped, and surveyed his family circle.

His mother, plumped down on the pneumatic blob of couch, had what he called her hurt look.

His father, sitting beside her, stared straight ahead. His mouth was pursed in a way that might have seemed grim in a bigger man.

Allisoun, sprawled on the resilient floor where it tilted up to merge with the wall at the other end of the room, looked doped. Her face was white, her eyelids red.

Willisoun, near her, studied Norm queerly. His fingers played with a cut flower, rolling and unrolling the petals, occasionally tugging one out.

Norm went over to the teletaction panel and plucked from the slot the newly engraved golden card bearing his death notice.

He studied the neat print. "You, Normsi" (there followed his citizenship number), "have been singled out by lot for a service of the highest honor that a citizen can render this world. You will . . ."

6

He heard an inane voice say, "Oh well, somebody has to get them," and realized that it was his own.

At that his mother reacted. She was on her feet and talking in a hoarsely agonized way, as if she'd been going on for half an hour, "You don't know what you're saying, Norm! It's horrible! Horrible! Don't you realize that you'll be . . . "

" . . . solely for the good of humanity, of course, and to avert far worse destruction . . . " his father put in hurriedly, apologetically.

" . . . Destroyed! Destroyed!" It was Allisoun who sobbed out the words, throwing her arms around him.

He looked at them warily—his mother gripping his arm, demanding attention, his father peering over her shoulder, Allisoun's soft hair pushing against his cheek, Willisoun keeping his distance.

He heard the inane voice say, "Oh well, that's war for you. Can't be helped."

"Don't say it!" his mother implored. "Oh, Norm, I can't bear to think of them taking you away. Why should it have to happen to us?"

His father was staring at the far wall, working his lips. " . . . And when he's so young, just starting life . . . " He muttered the words, as if accusing someone invisible.

"Don't let them, Norm," Allisoun sobbed into his neck.

"There's nothing you can do about it," the inane voice observed. He was beginning to hate its very sound.

His mother stood back. There were tears running down her cheeks.

"I won't let them take you," she said.

For a moment the others just looked at her. Then they caught fire from her spark.

"We'll fight them!" chimed his father, clenching his little fists and grinning spasmodically as he always did when he said anything in the least violent.

"Can't be done—" But the inane voice was swallowed up in a confused chorus of "We'll find ways,"

"You're ours, and we don't care what they do to us," and "Yes, by Man, we'll fight them!"

Allisoun said nothing, but she kept nodding her head against his chin and clung to him like death.

Willisoun dropped the half-stripped flower and shuffled up. "I've got influence," he said uneasily. "I'll see you get out. I won't let you down."

Suddenly the voices all stopped. In the silence Norm looked around. It occurred to him that they were waiting for him to say something. He looked around again. The faces wavered a little, but the look of anxious expectation stayed in the eyes. There was something embarrassing about that look.

"All right," he said quietly. "The worst they can do is kill me in disgrace instead of honor. I won't let them take me."

For a moment the significance of the dropped jaws, the raised eyebrows, didn't dawn on him. Even when Allisoun recoiled from him, lifting her tear-smeared disconcerted face.

Then it hit him.

His jaw tightened.

It was almost amusing to see the hasty, aggrieved way they began to backtrack, once he had called their bluff. His father began it.

"Now, Norm, I wouldn't do anything rash. We're all for you, my boy, of course, but there are so many things that have to be considered. It's terrible, I know, but the government has reasons for doing this thing—reasons which it's hard for a single individual to understand."

"Reasons for killing me?"

"Oh, it's ghastly when you put it that way, of course. But—did you hear Director M'Caslrai this afternoon?"

"No."

"You should have. He stressed that they were taking this step only with the greatest reluctance, after exploring every conceivable alternative. He emphasized that this time we'd managed to avoid war for a period of thirty-five years, longer than ever before—in itself a notable

8

accomplishment. But he pointed out that we dared not frustrate the mounting death-wish of mankind any longer. That death-wish is the realest thing in the world, Norm. It's the same guilt-urge that led thousands to confess to hideous crimes they never committed in the ancient witchcraft trials and political purges. It's the same hate-urge that piled pyramids of skulls before conquered cities and hills of human ashes before conquered countries. It's the thing that caused all past two-sided wars, with their messiness and inefficiency and their horrible unpredictability—their tendency to leap all bounds and engulf everyone. That inexorable death-wish, clearly indicated by the rocketing suicide and murder rates and a thousand other statistics, would inevitably break out in revolution or collective bestiality and probably, considering our degree of technical advancement, destroy all mankind—unless (as we have done successfully before—that's the big point!) unless we declare war."

"And he mentioned the religious side," his mother broke in, using what Norm called her hushed voice. "He said—" She choked a little but continued bravely, "—that Man the Hero must sacrifice himself to Man the Devil in order that Man the God may be able to go on."

"Oh that rot!"

She stepped back. Norm's father put his arm around her.

"I know what you're feeling, Norm," he said. "I was through it all myself, last time, and—"

"Were you picked?" Norm's voice was like a thrown rock.

"No, of course not—"

"Then you don't understand anything." He whirled on Willisoun. "I suppose they missed you too. Yes, of course they would. Bureaucracy's darling." As Willisoun bristled, Norm turned back to his parents.

"Let's get this straight now. Do you mean to tell me that you're willing to see my life snuffed out by war? Yes, Mother, I realize it's an intensely painful subject, but what I want to know is this: Do you think it's all right to kill fifty million people in order to save five billion from some possible greater injury? Don't look at me that way, Mother! I know I'm being crude and unkind, but it's the way I feel."

She lifted her head. Her lips trembled, but her voice was almost imploringly sweet as she said, "I know that no son of mine will do anything that will bring disgrace on himself and his family."

Her husband's arm tightened around her protectively, and the little man said, "Don't you see, Norm, you wouldn't be asked to do this unless it were absolutely necessary? Do you imagine I'd stand by without protesting if I thought it were? But the collective death-wish is a terrible thing and, as M'Caslrai kept hammering home, we've got to be realistic about it. We can only hold it in check by great sacrifices. For two hundred years we've been making those sacrifices. When absolutely necessary, we've declared war. But if we ever stopped . . . "

Norm snorted. "Do you believe everything M'Caslrai shoves down your throat? Can't you see that war is an inhuman device, a confession of failure, a throwback to the dirtiest superstitions? Men have been sacrificed before now to jealous gods and blood-hungry demons. Ever since history began, scapegoats have been selected and stoned. I wouldn't mind war against a tangible enemy—"

"What!" his mother interrupted. "Why, that would be horrible. To go out with hate in your heart and kill other people . . . "

"I can think of some cases in which it would be eminently worthwhile," said Norm harshly. "At least I'd get a run for my money. But this business of donating my body as a safety valve for man's destructive impulses—"

"But only to prevent worse destruction," his father cut in, his face contorted monkeywise in his eagerness to assuage. "It's only because any alternative would be far worse, that you're being called upon. It's to save people like your mother and Allisoun from indescribable horrors. I'm sure, Norm, that if you could see it in that light, you'd be only too willing—"

"To die? In order to preserve the present unholy setup that fattens on these sacrifices? To keep fossils like M'Caslrai in their present position?

For that's all it really comes down to—a conspiracy against the young men so they won't upset the old men's applecart."

"Now you're talking like you used to when you went with that radical crowd." His mother looked aggrieved. Then, shrewdly, "You talk that way about M'Caslrai because deep in your heart you look up to him. He's a great man. You wouldn't listen to him this afternoon because you were afraid he'd persuade you. And now you say anything nasty about him that comes into your head."

Her husband patted her arm. "We all said some foolish things in the peace days, Gret," he reminded her. "We weren't realistic. Lord, I wish we could still afford illusions. I'm sure you'd feel very differently, Norm, if only you'd seen the sincerity and suffering in M'Caslrai's face this afternoon." The little man's voice was placating, almost cheerful. His nervous smile had come back. Norm understood plainly: His father, always hating rows, figured that this one was over and the "smoothing out" time (his specialty) had arrived.

Norm watched him scamper spryly to the teletaction panel, heard him say, "Tell you what, they're re-teletacting M'Caslrai's address. You'll listen to it—eh, Norm?"

Feeling sick at his stomach, he hurried out of the room.

*

When he reached his bedroom he uncovered his ears, and was relieved to hear only an unintelligible sibilance of whispered conversation coming from the living room—none of those detestable, friendly, understanding, solemn mouthings of M'Caslrai.

It wasn't true, what his mother had said, he assured himself angrily. The World Director had no emotional hold on him. It was just that the man was such a boring, sanctimonious old hypocrite!

He repeated this to himself more than once as he stared at the blank bedroom wall.

THE WOLF PACK

The resilient floor was noiseless. He only became aware of Allisoun's presence a moment before her hand touched his shoulder. He let it stay there.

The room was dark except for a fan of dim light coming through the door and the ghostly glow outlining the furniture. The voices conferring out in the living room were muted to an unintelligible drone. It felt warm and stuffy and nauseous with flower-odors, like a funeral—the sweet stink of the weatherdome.

"Norm," said Allisoun softly, "you know how it is with those who go to war—"

"Yes?"

"They let them have whatever they want. Give them any Measure they desire."

"Well?"

"I was thinking that . . . well, you and I could be together, and sooner than we thought. We could do things and enjoy things that wouldn't be possible under other circumstances. We could have the sort of fun we had in our sex-introductory lessons—"

He turned around. The soft silhouetting light made her hair a bronze aureole around the darkness of her face. Her shoulders stood out whitely above her black slip.

"You'd like that, eh?" he asked.

Her "Yes" was almost inaudible.

"You'd really like it?"

She nodded. "And afterward . . . there'd be your son."

He surveyed her for a long moment. Then he reached for the white shoulders.

He pushed her back, held her at arm's length.

"So you'd like to be a hero's wife, eh?" he said loudly. "You'd get a thrill out of making love to a dead man? You'd like to be in on the orgies? You'd like to be one of the flower-decked concubines of the petted one who next year will have his heart torn out on a primeval God's stone altar?

12

You'd like to count the remaining moments gloatingly? You'd like to bear a dead man's son for the next general bloodletting? Well, I wouldn't like it."

Willisoun stumbled into the room. "Look here," he blatted, snatching at Norm, "you can't talk to my sister that way."

"Oh yes I can." He shoved Willisoun against the bed and walked back into the living room. By the time Willisoun had followed him out, he was standing with his back to the outer door. He stopped Willisoun with a gesture and looked around—at his father with upraised hands fluttering the air, his mother slumped on the couch like a sick cow, Allisoun in the shadow of the opposite doorway, her brother a little ahead of her, face flushed and hands clenched.

"I'll say my say and then get out," Norm told them. "Maybe I'm doing the wrong thing. Maybe I'm just showing myself up as selfish and ignorant. I know that there are times when the few must perish for the sake of the many—when we must have a 'finest hour' and a goriest, most glorious day. I know there are a lot of things we don't understand, especially about human nature. Maybe I ought to let myself be destroyed gladly. Maybe war is the greatest social invention since Brotherly Love. Maybe it's magnificent long-range thinking and M'Caslrai's a benign genius. Maybe in view of the ugliness of human nature, it's the only alternative to universal chaos.

"But if that's the way human nature works, I don't want any part of it. Oh, I know I should have thought of all this before, and that it looks as if I were squealing just because I happened to be the one who drew the unlucky number. But better late than never! I decline to perform the service requested of me. I'll use any means to avoid performing it. And I'll urge others to do the same. Good-by, folks, I'm cutting loose."

Willisoun walked toward him stiff-legged. "You won't get far, you cowardly . . . "

Norm's right to the jaw connected. Willisoun hit the tilted floor-section, bounced, came to rest. His fogged eyes, glaring crookedly at Norm, were half-moons of sick hate. Groping for support, his hands happened to close on the flower he had dropped earlier. Fingers and thumb squeezed the remaining petals to mush.

Norm turned and walked out.

At the togs-rack he jerked on his walking clothes, automatically transferring his death notice from hand to hand. A blast of chill air cut his face as he left the weatherdome, but he did not pull down his veil.

A red sunset struck golden glints from the fantastic, cloud-piercing spires of the New City, made a golden pillar to heaven of Supracenter, whence M'Caslrai might even now be looking paternalistically down. Norm turned his back on that fancied gaze and headed for the Old City's ragged, low skyline, blackly silhouetted by the angry rays.

A half-hour's furious walking carried him out of the interurban green belt with its bizarre mingling of weatherdomes and winter. The tree-lined avenues gave way to steep-walled canyons, through which the wind dipped and tore. Resilient plastic pavement of a relatively recent date blotted out the distinction between sidewalk and street, as no vehicular traffic was permitted in these narrow ways. Occasional roofs, however, had been adapted as landing stages for riding sticks and copters.

There were people abroad. All over the world, old city populations were dropping, and there was talk of clearing them out altogether. But individuals clung to these outmoded, time-hallowed warrens, the more tenaciously as it became possible to live a more isolated life in them. Not everyone relished the highly paced and socialized existence of the new city skylons.

Unconsciously Norm increased his alertness. One thing M'Caslrai was supposed to have said this afternoon was quite true: the murder rate had soared fantastically—and the Old City was a Mecca for deviants and discontents.

Every night brought its quota of killings and assaults, most of them purposeless outbursts of cruelty and lust, as if all the Jack-the-Rippers of the past had been reincarnated a hundredfold. Everyone was suspect. The gray-garbed police Norm passed were too ostentatious in their disregard of him, and once or twice he got the impression he was being followed.

He paid no particular attention. His mind kept chewing on the scene that had occurred back home; rehearsing it again and again—sometimes in its rightful setting, sometimes against a background of darkness, sometimes against a magnified ghostly version of M'Caslrai's gaunt, homely, reproachful face—until the lesser faces of his family circle became the painful, too vivid distortions of an olden time surrealist painter, with personalities to match. Gret, his mother, sunk most of the time in a kind of heavy brooding that almost cut her off from the world; hungrily affectionate yet completely unsympathetic, taking all emotion for her province and no one else's. Jon, his father, whittled by timidity down to the tiniest shred of a man, driven frantic by the slightest friction, living in a painstakingly fabricated dream-world where his decisions amounted to something. Allisoun, constantly veering between a hysterical romance-fed primness and an equally hysterical love-thirst. Willisoun, superficially more adjusted than the rest, with his important, quietly mysterious government job, but alternating his hail-fellow-well-met manner with a surliness that might hide anything—Norm couldn't forget the diseased hate that had been in his eyes at the last and the way his hand had closed on the flower.

A panorama from which past centuries peered out more and more often, slipped by half-noticed as he pushed deeper and deeper into the Old City. Walls of brick and stone, patched here and there with panels of glastic indicating still-inhabited dwelling units. Rusted vents that might be the remains of pre-electronic air-conditioning systems. Boxes overhead that had housed microwave traffic control systems. Once he went down an alleyway paved with a worn stone-substitute, and occasionally the fringe of his attention strayed to dusty windows that looked suspiciously like ancient glass.

As he turned out of the alleyway into a scarcely wider street, he met a small hurrying figure in green walking togs. He brushed past her, but she turned and stared at him closely after a quick glance at his gloved left

15

hand. For a moment impulse and prudence fought in her narrowly elfin face. Then she turned and followed him.

She was not Norm's only follower. Another, taller and more darkly clad, melted back into the alleyway at her appearance, then after a moment continued his hungrily striding pursuit, avoiding the broad luminescent bands on pavement and walls. Except for the ghostly light cast by those stripes, it was becoming rapidly darker.

Gradually and silently, the two pursuers closed in. The one farther back took something thin and bright from his pouch, held it so that it was masked by his forearm.

Suddenly, at the mouth of another and darker alleyway, Norm stopped. He had come to a decision about the four faces leering in his mind.

"They're insane," he said aloud, lifting his clenched hands, "The whole pack of them."

A golden gleam caught his attention. He realized that he had been clutching his death notice all this time. He held it up to the phosphorescent wall-band.

It was his passport back to respectability. By means of it he could still be reconciled with his family and associates, still die with honor. It symbolized the fact that it was not too late to turn back.

He took it between his fingers and prepared to rip it across.

Someone touched his arm. He jerked around. He vaguely remembered having passed this girl in green a few corners back, but now for the first time he saw her slim face, her oddly animated eyes. Something tugged at his memory.

"You said you think they're all insane?" she asked softly.

He nodded doubtfully. He didn't understand how she could know to whom he was referring.

An unusual look, an evil joyful look, came into her eyes which never left his face. She smiled slyly and leaned forward. After a considerable pause she whispered.

"You're right. They are all insane. You and I too. The whole world is crazy. The only difference is that you and I know."

For an extraordinary moment the only things Norm could see clearly were her strange fey eyes. Everything else was darkly rocking. The floor of his mind had tilted and the ideas were slipping, sliding.

"You believe that?" she whispered.

Norm realized that he was nodding his head.

She laughed. "Then you'd better not tear up your death notice," she said. "You may find a better use for it."

It is hard to say what made Norm whirl around again at that moment. Hardly a noise, for the attack, though swift, was horribly soundless. Perhaps he got his cue from a movement of the air, or a doubly reflected gleam from the blade gripped in the second follower's hand.

But whirl he did, and simultaneously duck, and the blade, abruptly glowing as if white-hot, drove just over his shoulder, inches from his face.

Hardly losing a moment in recovering, the dark attacker ripped sidewise at the girl.

But Norm was swift too, as if his subconscious had long been preparing for this. He caught hold of a fold of dark fabric and jerked. The glowing blade sliced air in front of the green girl's throat.

Riding with the jerk, the attacker swung around with a serpentine swiftness, like a murderer in a nightmare, and stabbed out at his victim.

But Norm caught the knife hand and drove blow after blow at the black-swathed jaw, unmindful of the fingers that tried to pry his loose and of the electron-edged blade that twitched at his undersleeve, slicing the tough fabric to ribbons.

He felt the figure weaken. He set his feet and drove home a solider blow.

Sparking as it hit, the knife dropped to the pavement. The figure slumped, sprawled full length across one of the phosphorescent bands.

Norm bent over it. Faintly in his ears, a police-screech echoed. The girl tugged at his sleeve, saying, "Why did he . . . ? Do you know who he is?"

THE WOLF PACK

Yet when Norm pulled aside the black veil, it was the girl who whispered, "Willisoun!"

The police-screech sounded clearer. A search-beam probed up and down.

The girl said, "They mustn't find us."

Norm was fumbling around on his hands and knees.

"Come on!" The girl caught hold of his sleeve.

The search-beam found them. The screech came three times, rapidly.

"Please!" The girl was trying to drag him toward the alleyway. "If you're what I think you are, and if you're willing to trust me at all—"

But it was because Norm did trust her—and remembered what she had said—that he delayed. Scooping up the fallen gold death notice, he jumped to his feet. Together they hurried down the dark alleyway.

CHAPTER II

There was little sleep as that night went around the world. In scattered offices weary-eyed actuaries fed information tapes into machines for a last check on their figures. It was not only the number of war deaths that must be accurately calculated, (and if they calculated one too many, they were morally guilty of murder), but also the exact amounts of material slated for destruction. There were thousands of factors that must never be lost sight of. Some were real, such as prices, availability, production and transportation costs, statistics on total expenditures from the last wars. Some were arbitrary, such as the equating of so many wounded casualties to one death, or the substitution of raw for processed materials. While some were frank extrapolations, such as the regrettable necessity for allowing for the greater destruction made possible by modern technology. Although this factor must of course be shaved as much as possible, it would never do to overlook it completely.

Elsewhere, electronic wheels were set in motion that would result in sharply upped transmutation, synthesizing, processing, and agricultural production. Auxiliary power plants were opened. Amazingly dispersed munitions factories began to take form. The first of the great triphibian transports started down the production line.

Teletaction made it possible for major and minor executives all over the world to hold thousands of conferences as efficiently and comfortably as if each conferring group were together in the same room—and, indeed, it gave just that effect. Arrangements for a quarter-billion job transfers were smoothly concluded. Priorities on critical materials were argued out. Psychologists put the finishing touches on courses of orientation for death. Deadlines were determined for putting into effect a complete system of civilian rationing, for a period of belt-tightening was a profoundly necessary part of the war.

Various entertainment-chains and vice-rings, openly encouraged or at least winked at by police authorities, prepared for expanded activities.

THE WOLF PACK

Religion, which had turned its back on God and devoted itself to the worship of man and man's destiny, likewise laid plans.

In a billion homes the lights stayed on. In one out of twenty there was numbing shock, hopeless horror, agonized grief, unanswerable questionings, spasms of rebellion. In the other nineteen there was a feeling of relief so intense as to preclude sleep, mingled with stern self-questionings and an uneasy sense of guilt.

Everywhere was mounting nervous tension, which would hold for months, until the thing was over. Despite this, scattered experts scanning the hourly statistics gave vent to long-anticipated sighs of relief, as they saw the suicide rate drop almost to zero and the murder and assault rates swoop almost as low. Mankind had something bigger to worry about than personal miseries and ecstasies and compulsions.

If there was any single emotion that came close to being universal, that touched both the high and the low, those on the spot and those off it, it was fear—an irrational, nerve-tightening dread. More than a century had passed since the last true conflict, but the sense of an enemy lingered subconsciously, to be revived when the war-patterns were reestablished. Odd noises and odors brought quickening heartbeats. Men who walked or flew abroad looked over their hunched shoulders, as if expecting the plunge of the robot bomb or the blue stab of the ray or the silent snowfall of radioactive death. Men on shipboard scanned the empty waters, as if expecting them to be broken, stealthily or with a convulsive splash, by the emerging of a murder-bent triphibian. Men inside were troubled by an uneasiness about the lights, as if all those bright windows on the night side of Earth formed too conspicuous a beacon for some unknown foe lurking in the depths of space.

CHAPTER III

In world Director M'Caslrai's office atop Supracenter there was a total absence of bustle and noise, as was perhaps appropriate at the focal point of all this activity. No lights blinked, no secretary-machines hummed, no color-changing maps and graphs troubled the cool gray of the walls, no distant subordinates appeared in teletactive counterpart seeking okays or advice. M'Caslrai was alone.

His tall, tired, gangling frame was relaxed. Superficially his face was tranquil. It was a big brooding face, seamed with significant wrinkles. As capable of stern decision as of drollery, but somehow always genial. A face on which history was clearly written. The face of a man who knew men, and how to handle them.

In the whole room, only one thing moved: M'Caslrai's gnarled forefinger. Back and forth it scratched an inch of chair-arm. Back and forth. Back and forth.

He looked like a great leader who, after a momentous decision, permits himself the painful luxury of weighing his actions for a last time, of asking himself whether he could possibly have taken any other course, of toting up the suffering his decision would cause against the suffering it had averted.

And yet, beneath the surface, there was something shockingly wrong in the picture M'Caslrai presented. A certain uncouthness of posture may have had something to do with it, a hint of stiffness in the dark garments. Yet those were only details. You couldn't put your finger on the main cause. But whatever that was, there was a sense of monstrous hidden abnormality about the man, the persistent suggestion that M'Caslrai was profoundly out of place—either in space, or time.

He did not look up as J'Wilobe entered unannounced. The slim, lean-jawed Secretary of Dangers had an expression that would have seemed fretful, had it not been so intense. Again there was that instant impression of abnormality, but with J'Wilobe its cause was not obscure. You felt you were looking at the human counterpart of a highly intelligent hybrid of lemur and ferret—a super-Goebbels.

His gaze roved suspiciously to either side as he came through the door. He paced back and forth for a few moments biting his lip, then let fall, "I found another of those damned chess sets."

M'Caslrai stirred, slowly rubbed his dark-guttered eyelids.

"Makes three in a week," J'Wilobe continued in staccato bursts. "I destroyed it, of course, but it shook me up. Obviously, someone knows I could have been the greatest chess-player in the world." He threw back his head. "Knows I gave up the game to devote myself wholly to government—couldn't serve two masters. Knows what a vice chess is. Knows how I'm still tempted. Leaves the sets around to upset me. Knows what the sight of one does to me."

He continued to pace.

M'Caslrai raised his tangled eyebrows.

"Mister J'Wilobe . . . " he began, waggling a forefinger at the Secretary of Dangers.

J'Wilobe stared intently at the extended digit. His lean arms tightened against his sides. His face paled a trifle.

M'Caslrai made a fist of his hand. "Your pardon, sir," he said, smiling humbly. "I had forgotten your . . . idiosyncrasy. But to continue. You're getting at something bigger than the chessmen?"

J'Wilobe faced him. "Right! The chessmen are only a single minor instance. I can put my finger on . . . I mean, point out . . . I mean, designate, a hundred comparable cases. Could have told you weeks ago, except I wanted to be absolutely sure. It's so unlikely, you see. But unlikely or not, the evidence is overwhelming. We are up against an organized underground opposition, the methods and like of which . . . "

M'Caslrai raised his hand. "One moment, Mister J'Wilobe. I believe that this matter you are about to expound is of the highest significance. I think it best, therefore, that we call in the others."

J'Wilobe pressed his lips together, shook his head.

"Inscra and Heshifer at a minimum," M'Caslrai pressed.

J'Wilobe shrugged an unwilling consent. While M'Caslrai used the teletactor, he stepped outside and signaled to a bruised-jawed young man who was fingering a cut flower.

"You're in shape for a job tonight, Willisoun?" he asked.

Willisoun nodded.

"Any word as yet on the thugs who assaulted you in the Old City?"

Willisoun shook his head.

"I dislike men who run into danger," said J'Wilobe. "Be more cautious in the future. Regarding your present assignment, a secret conference is about to be held in M'Caslrai's office. When it breaks up, hold yourself in readiness to follow anyone whom I designate. Remember, it may be anyone—even M'Caslrai. And be sure to make yourself invisible. You too frequently neglect that precaution. I dislike careless men."

When he returned, M'Caslrai was busying himself taking a box out of a cabinet, setting it on his desk. The World Director went out of his way to pull forward a chair, so that there were four arranged at comfortable distances around the desk. His movements were tired and slow, but suggested reservoirs of inward strength.

Inscra arrived first by a matter of moments. The General Secretary was an expressionless, ponderous individual, who always seemed to be moving through a denser medium than air. Only his eyes looked alive, and even there one could not be sure that the animating force was life.

Secretary of Minds Heshifer was almost the exact opposite. A small man, ridiculously spry for one so aged, with bald head and a bushy white beard. Fussy, pedantic, quick-witted, expression always ashift.

M'Caslrai welcomed them with a friendly gesture. Then he opened the box and lifted out a bottle.

The movement dislodged a tiny grey something which scuttled across the desk. No one else reacted, but Inscra jerked back with a convulsive gasp.

Heshifer captured the something with a flick of his hand, as though it were an insect. "A scrap of memo tape," he remarked, looking. No one said anything, though it was with difficulty that Inscra tore his gaze away from Heshifer's half-closed hand.

M'CasIrai carefully tilted the bottle. From the seemingly sealed neck an amber liquid poured.

"Afterward you can serve yourself, gentlemen," he said, indicating the four glasses with courtly awkwardness. "Mister J'Wilobe has something to tell us."

Hand shaking a little, Inscra tossed his drink. Heshifer sipped appreciatively. J'Wilobe lifted his to his lips, sniffed it, looked around suspiciously, hesitated, set it down.

"You all know that there are forces working against us," he began abruptly. "Though some of you don't like to admit it." He glared at Heshifer, who shrugged blithely. "Secret, underground forces, bent on upsetting the social order, on destroying the present government, and especially on sabotaging the war. There is evidence that similar forces were active to some degree during past wars. They could have been brought into the open long before this, if there had not been so much objection in some quarters to the unlimited questioning of suspects which I urged—the employment of emotional urging and similar methods of persuasion."

"You know I do not like to see people treated that way," said M'CasIrai gently. "Though, of course, if the safety of the world and the glory of Man are at stake . . . and if there is a threat to the young men who are giving up their lives . . . "

"Naturally any opposition must be liquidated," said Inscra sharply, "if it exists."

J'Wilobe smiled. "The opposition exists. It is only the strangeness of its methods—the puzzling quality of its stratagems—that keeps most individuals from becoming aware of it." He looked around with a veiled contemptuousness, then said suddenly, "Who would suspect—gifts? I mean, if the gifts were perfectly okay and each happened to be the thing its recipient most wanted. Yet gifts can be deadly. You don't give drink to a drunkard just before the day's work. Especially you don't give it to a reformed drunkard. Nevertheless, within the past two weeks dozens of such 'gifts' have been made, always anonymously, to some of our highest executives and most trusted subordinates. There is, in my own case, a matter of chess sets."

Heshifer muttered something that ended with " . . . as impossible as telepathy," then snorted, "If that's all you have to tell us——"

"It's only a beginning. Next among these nuisance tactics of the opposition, conies—voices. Voices in the dark or over dark teletactors, voices dubbed into reading tapes, unplaceable voices heard for a moment in crowds—all reminding the individual of unpleasant incidents that happened in his childhood, incidents he wants to forget, or incidents that never happened but that the voice is trying to convince him did.

"Yet another secret weapon—monotony. Lights that begin to blink, sounds that begin to drone, taped words and sentences that repeat themselves over and over.

"Think how such 'harmless' means can be used to distract men, to upset them, to ruin their efficiency!

"Finally, something you all know about—this epidemic of what we've called convulsive accidents. Cases of mild poisoning and electric shock, with the victim suffering muscular spasms and going into a hazy and unrealistic mental state that sometimes lasts for days. There have been altogether too many of those 'accidents.' It's as if there were a silent wolf pack around us—dozens of the red-eyed beasts——"

He broke off to look at Inscra. The General Secretary had just given an abrupt nod, and his eyes looked more than ever alive—or whatever it was. His voice was like them.

"I think I see what you're getting at, J'Wilobe. I've come across similar cases myself, and I believe now that you are right in considering them significant. What is more, I can add another type of occurrence. Several workers in one of my subdepartments have been troubled by what we called overtiredness. They gradually become slow in their movements, their eyes seem to glaze, they go into what you could describe as a mild trance.

THE WOLF PACK

In that trance they give utterance to irresponsible, foolish ideas. For brief hazy periods, they doubt things which should not be ever doubted—even war. I have paid no attention—these days, a certain amount of mental fatigue is taken for granted. In one case, though, I remember that an analysis of the blood happened to be made, and traces of a primitive chemical noted—lysergic acid. I thought nothing of it at the time, but now . . . "

He broke off and restlessly reached for the bottle—just at the moment Heshifer happened to do likewise. The smaller man was ahead of him, so Inscra set his glass on the table. As Heshifer picked up the bottle, the small gray thing fluttered from his hand to the floor. Instantly Inscra shrank back, repeating his former erratic behavior. There was a moment of confusion. Heshifer set his foot on the thing, muttered a quick "I'm sorry," stooped, picked it up, shoved it in his pouch. Then he poured the drinks, handing Inscra his.

As they settled back, M'Caslrai spoke. He had been sprawling back in his armchair, listening carefully, making no comment.

"Mister J'Wilobe, that's a mighty interesting matter you've been narrating to us, and one we've got to act on right quick, but I don't think you've quite got the hang of it. You see what's happening—and you're right in thinking that it's hostile. Yes, you can bet you are—but you don't yet see the why."

With almost a twinkle in his eye, he turned to Heshifer. "I'd have thought you'd have spotted it. After all, you're Secretary of Minds. But no, it would be unfair to expect any of you to get it. I never would myself, except I like to poke around in the byways of history. And that's where you have to poke this time, boys—way back in the twentieth century, old reckoning. Mighty interesting times . . . though not as much as the nineteenth. . . . "

His voice was both droll and dead serious as he continued, "In those days they didn't treat deviants and eccentrics as we do now. They had a lot of queer methods, some barbaric, some rather fanciful. I happened to read up on them. They had a thing called hypnotism, a little like our mental persuasion. A way of opening someone's mind to suggestion, chiefly through the skillful use of monotony.

"Then there was psychoanalysis—a prying into the depths of the victim's mind; a searching for his earliest experiences, to be used as levers to change his attitudes.

"Occupational therapy was another. Like the other methods, they used it on the people they called insane. It was a matter of getting the person to do something he liked to do, something that would occupy his mind—you presented him with a well-chosen 'gift.'

"Mustn't forget shock treatment, of course. That was a prime favorite of theirs for the insane, and pretty barbaric. Electric or chemical shock, to dredge up forgotten thoughts and emotions.

"Or what they called truth serums. Chemicals designed to let down inhibitions, to make the victim speak out his hidden thoughts.

"Reckon you get it, gentlemen?"

The silence lasted. Inscra looked stupefied. Heshifer half-befuddled, half-incredulous. While J'Wilobe's reaction was closer to anger.

"Do you mean to tell me that the opposition thinks we are 'insane'?" J'Wilobe pronounced the archaic word distastefully.

M'Caslrai nodded. "That's the way I figure it."

"And they're treating us as such? Trying to 'cure' us?"

"That's about the size of it, Mister J'Wilobe," said M'Caslrai mildly.

"But . . . but . . . " The thick, mumbly quality of Inscra's words focused attention on him. He looked more than stupefied now. He looked drugged.

"What I want to know . . . " He stumbled again.

"His eyes!" breathed J'Wilobe. "The truth serum!"

Over them, a few minutes ago so unpleasantly alive, there had fallen a veil.

He managed to finish:

" . . . is, are we really? I mean, are we really insane? Tell me, someone, are we?"

27

CHAPTER IV

The entry-indicator blinked as Heshifer bustled into the limited elevator.
"Anyone in your family get a death notice?" he asked conversationally.
The fat operator shook his head. "But I got a nephew who did."
Heshifer clucked sympathetically.

"He's a crazy kid," the operator volunteered. "Be the making of him, except . . ."

"Yes, of course," said Heshifer gently and leaped into abstraction.

Plummeting from the eyrie atop Supracenter toward the deepest basement, the elevator accelerated, then achieved such a smooth and steady speed that it seemed to stop.

The Secretary of Minds looked the perfect pedant. Judging from his vague eyes, pursed lips, and jutting beard, he might have been thinking of something highly obscure or of nothing at all—in no case anything practical.

He swung around. Save for himself and the operator, the cage was empty. Restlessly he walked to the stair, popped up far enough to survey the second floor of the elevator.

With a shrug he resumed his meditations. But one might have noticed the faintest of frowns troubling his tufty white eyebrows.

The elevator stopped. Again the indicator blinked as, with an amiable but abstracted nod, Heshifer stepped out and turned sharply to the left.

The operator craned his neck curiously and took a step sideways—then recoiled, clutching his shoulder.

There had been no second passenger, the indicator had not blinked, but his eyes, watching the resilient flooring a few paces behind Heshifer, filled with horror. In a panic of haste he shut the door and started back up.

Like a self-important little mole returning to his lair, Heshifer hurried along the lonely corridor until he reached the insulated precincts of the Deep Mental Lab. As he scuttled through the file room, he blinked familiarly at the clerks, who were busy getting taped transcripts of brainwave records for mental dossiers of deviants and troublemakers. A large number of such dossiers were being requested by psychologists at war-reception centers.

Inside his private office, Heshifer's manner changed. The blink and bustle dropped away, leaving a soft-footed, enigmatic watchfulness. After a few minutes efficiently spent in teletacting requests and instructions, he slipped through an inner door.

He had gone fifty feet down a narrow gray corridor when, without warning, he swung around. This time he did not bother to mask the suspicious frown. For ten seconds he stood motionless, his eyes roving over the empty corridor behind him, his ears drinking in the faintest sounds. Arriving at a decision, he returned to his office and searched it thoroughly. Then he set auxiliary electronic locks on the outer and inner doors and, with a shrug, started once more down the narrow corridor.

He did not notice the faint imprints that appeared and disappeared in the flooring a dozen feet behind him.

After a short walk he paused and traced with his forefinger a design on the blank wall. He ducked through the doorway that suddenly yawned.

The secondary corridor descended at a gentle angle. Some hundred feet from the entrance a barely audible clink brought him to a stop. A section of wall beside him became transparent, revealing a young, vigilant face.

"The tunnel's clear?" asked Heshifer.

The watcher nodded.

"All electronic barriers set? No visitants for the Old City ahead of me? No indications of spy-beams?"

More nods answered him.

"Thanks, doc," said Heshifer.

The transparency became a blank wall. Heshifer hurried on.

The imprints followed him. There was no clink as they passed the critical point.

Heshifer emerged on a small platform in a chamber of moderate size. Beyond the platform were two gleaming metallic troughs, which led off side by side, into the mouths of twin tunnels. In the troughs were cradled a number of small cylindrical vehicles.

Heshifer opened the port of the nearest and climbed in. Almost silently, with swift smooth acceleration, the vehicle glided into the tunnel and whisked out of sight.

Nothing happened for perhaps a dozen seconds. Then—no one appeared, but the port of the second vehicle opened and, after a brief pause, closed. Softly the vehicle started forward.

CHAPTER V

Norm looked up doubtfully at the girl in green. He was still uncertain whether to take her idly-tossed revelations as confetti or grenades. Coming here had been a confusion of screeching alleys, ruinous basements, ambiguous passageways, a careening ride inside a metal mole, until he had stumbled out into the final surprise of soft silent corridors lined with flowers. His mind still fluoresced with it.

Nevertheless he was sure of one thing: that he felt more at home in this strange little subterranean room than he ever had in his own dwelling.

The girl in green swung her legs from a table near the archway. It was obvious that she was aware of their trimness. She looked at him innocently, like an elf on the witness stand.

"You mean," he fumbled, "that you consider yourselves attendants in one huge insane asylum?"

She grinned approvingly. "Except that the lunatics hold the balance of power. And so we have to walk very softly. Or else—it really doesn't matter—we're the insane ones, bent on warping the minds of the majority. We're monomaniacs on the topic, I warn you of that. And with all the languorousness of monomaniacs." She suddenly looked at him like a short-haired cat. "What's the matter anyway? Beginning to doubt that a world which devised war could be anything but insane?"

"Of course not, but in spite of what you started to say about your organization's long historical background, it all seems so . . . "

"Hit or miss? We don't live up to your idea of a powerful secret society?"

"I guess that's what I mean."

She smiled.

"But look at the casual way you picked me up and started to tell me things," he protested. "How do you know I won't betray you?"

"You'd prefer a lot of mumbo-jumbo—oaths, tests, initiations?" she inquired solicitously. "It wouldn't occur to you, I suppose, that we might have been watching you for a long time? Or that any organization is strong only insofar as it can act on the spur of the moment?"

"Yes, but . . . "

"And, as for betraying us, where are we now?"

"Under the Old City."

"But where?"

"I don't know. It was dark, and there were those crazy tunnels."

"Exactly. And who am I?"

"You said to call you J'Quilvens."

"Yes, but who am I? Where would you find me?"

"I don't know."

"You see. You wouldn't make such a valuable traitor after all." She smoothed her green slip. "Besides we have reason to trust you. You passed a test when we first met."

He shook his head. He was beginning to like her very much. "You're wrong there. I was just fighting in self-defense. And Willisoun wasn't after you."

She smiled. "You've a lot to learn about your precious potential brother-in-law. You didn't even know that he worked for J'Wilobe.

"He's quite a problem child, Willisoun," she added dreamily. Then, after a moment, "You're in love with his sister?"

"Look," said Norm quickly, "you were going to tell me about the background of your movement."

J'Quilvens smiled, lit two smolder-sticks, tossed him one, leaned back, sniffing the aromatic smoke, and casually began. Very much like a small girl uttering whatever fancies came into her head—the muse of history's brat tattling.

"It started in the twentieth century, old reckoning. There was still some insight then into the psychological state of the world. It was before the big propaganda engines went wild—and a person still had some idea of what was coming into his mind and from where. They realized that certain nations were for all practical purposes insane—paranoid, regressive, schizoid.

"But the larger truth was ignored. Only a few men realized that abnormal psychology was far more fruitful than the normal variety for the simple reason that it was truer. That from the beginning man had behaved abnormally, believing fiercely in things that didn't exist, positing all sorts of weird forces for which there wasn't a grain of evidence, exalting his prejudices and eccentricities, his little private experiences, into vast, cosmic fabrics of morality. That to a large extent all civilization was just one gigantic case history.

"Of those few doubtful men, a handful happened to contact each other. They shared their insights and grew a little more certain of their ground. They said, 'We're not like ordinary psychiatrists, who seek only to make sound maniacs out of sick maniacs. We presume to view man against the cosmic background, his littleness and misery and hunger, his boastings and cringings, his tricks and pretenses, his terrors and hallucinations, his kickings and squirmings, his shrieks and snarls. We want to teach him to laugh at himself. And someday, in spite of himself, we'll drive him sane!'"

For a moment Norm felt that she was looking through him.

Then, leaning forward, lightly resting elbows on knees, she continued quietly, "Whenever they had the time and opportunity—for all of them were tied to irksome routines—they investigated. Some of them studied the modern symptoms of the world's madness, probed the symbolic mass-dreams hidden in art, propaganda, and advertising. Others concentrated on the traumas that had occurred while mankind was groping from barbarism to civilization—the wars, enslavements, and superstitious delusions that had warped civilization's childhood. Still others tried to determine the prognosis of the ailment.

"The prognosis was negative. Society took several wrong turns. Under the pressure of a ruthless new puritanism, the promising spirit of scientific skepticism was mummified into learned specialities. Basic questions were dodged so often that a general inferiority complex came into existence. Pretense took the place of progress. Fear was enthroned.

"At times the tiny enlightened minority met to exchange their augmented information. Differences of opinion rose. Some boldly attempted to set up the psychiatry of history as a new branch of knowledge. This resulted in a split. Those who resisted realized that their knowledge would merely be assimilated into the general insanity and become a worthless pedantry. As indeed happened—you can still find traces in the present philosophy that a certain degree of irrational eccentricity, within strict social limits, is desirable."

Norm nodded. She continued lightly, almost humorously, as if too much seriousness were dangerous. "Times changed. There came the first and second world leagues, the first and second world federations, the all-out Nuclear War that reduced Earth's population to a fraction of one percent, the reclaiming of the Deathlands, the rule of the Benevolent Lunatics—we aren't the only crazy ones, Norm—the re-pioneering of the planets.

"The main group kept working in secret. At intervals, after the carefullest consideration, new members were admitted.

"The organization shifted with the times, responsive to winds of influence. Sometimes it was almost open; sometimes, when suspicious tyranny was enthroned, it was secret—though there were times, I imagine, when it survived solely because no policeman or politician would take it seriously—it inclined to such long-range views that it seldom became involved in practical action. And that," she added bitterly "is not entirely a past matter.

"Sometimes the members considered it little more than a nonsensical hobby. Sometimes they were almost dead serious. Sometimes there were bursts of activity—meetings, discussions, plans. Sometimes they were a wolf pack, nipping at man's heels and almost forgetting not to snap at the jugular vein—a lot of them weren't humanity-lovers, believe me! Sometimes members lost touch with each other for decades, almost for lifetimes.

"They never had a real name. Sometimes they called themselves the Company of the Sane, or the League of Psychiatrists. They got into the habit of addressing each other as 'doctor' or 'geodoc' because the world was their patient.

"Times continued to change. The world state was born and the worship of man. War as we know it today came into existence—not, like you've been taught to believe, as the result of logical analysis, but because a civil-war army, sworn to suicide in case of failure, thought they'd been trapped before the war began and jumped the gun on self-destruction.

"The final, fixed phase in the psychosis of history had set in. The docs half woke from their centuries of dabbling and realized that they could no longer evade the problem facing them. Though their organization was almost at its lowest ebb, the time had come to act.

"In the face of a socialization, regimentation, and surveillance more intense than any they had faced before, they went back to the practices of their secretest days—and improved on them. If they had gone underground before, this time they really burrowed. Elaborate precautions were taken to prevent infiltration by spies. A cell-system was set up, to avoid too much mutual acquaintance of members.

"Cautiously they began to experiment at influencing the world. Sometimes they worked on individuals, sometimes on groups. They tried out all the psychological and secret propaganda techniques that had been developed through the ages, discarding, reviving, improving, inventing. They perfected their methods, gathered data, distributed their members in the most effective pattern for action.

"Wars, being the most tragic of mankind's symptoms, were their chief target. Each war they opposed with every weapon they dared use. Each time they planned and put into effect elaborate psychological counterprograms.

"And yet each time they failed. Wars marched on relentlessly. The counterprograms always dissolved into futile nuisance tactics. Each generation produced its quota of sacrificial deaths. Until now . . . "

THE WOLF PACK

A silvery tone sounded from beyond the archway. J'Quilvens reacted to it, but did not break off. Her eyes burned, there were spots of color in her cheeks, her lips were tight lines. For a moment the elf was a fury.

"And now . . . we know that we dare not let this war succeed. If we fail, it's the finish. We've studied our own symptoms as well as those of the world. If we fail, we'll merely become an integral part of the universal madness—a futile counter-symptom. We've been too careful, been too much afraid for our own skins, perhaps we've secretly gloried in our position as the only sane persons in an insane world. We've got to take chances, try every method, fight!"

"Did I hear someone mention that irrational word?" a cool voice inquired.

A tall shaven-headed man in amber pajamas was standing in the archway. He was handsome, after the fashion of an ancient Eastern god—aloof, faintly amused, coldly compassionate.

J'Quilvens turned slowly. "I did, F'Sibr."

"He has arrived," he informed her. He looked at Norm, who began to feel uncomfortable.

"I'm coming." J'Quilvens dropped from the table. "Wait here," she told Norm.

The shaven-headed man gave Norm another unrevealing look and followed her out.

CHAPTER VI

"They're on to us," Heshifer affirmed, his white beard wagging. "This time J'Wilobe's paranoid delusions coincide with reality. And M'Caslrai actually spotted our aims and the sources of our methods."

"And yet you're sure you weren't followed." F'Sibr inquired unperturbedly.

"Impossible! As impossible as telepathy!" Heshifer grinned. "Oh, I'll admit my suspicions were roused for a moment, but it wasn't anything. The electronic barriers were all in order."

"You have a weakness for running risks," said F'Sibr mildly. "That business of the chess sets was injudicious. And putting the truth drug into Inscra's drink was impudently foolhardy."

"But don't you see, we've got to be foolhardy!" J'Quilvens broke in eagerly.

"And it did shake them up so beautifully," Heshifer added, smiling reminiscently.

They were conferring in a low, large, comfortably furnished room from which several corridors radiated. There were softly glowing three-dimensional pictures, bits of sculpture, bunches of flowers, as if a conscious effort had been made to suppress any feeling of underground grimness or of wide-webbed, long-tentacled efficiency.

F'Sibr sat, arms folded. Heshifer paced, sometimes almost skipping, as if trying to keep up with the sudden twists and turns of his thoughts. J'Quilvens perched, playing with a smolder-stick.

"I see no reason to put our general plan in jeopardy," said F'Sibr. "The masked trend toward sanity is increasing as calculated. The propaganda of doubt and distrust, foolproof and insanity-proof by test, is successfully invading every phase of the war. The master propaganda—"

Heshifer picked up a fragile jar of reddish powder and tossed it in his hand. "What's this?"

37

THE WOLF PACK

"A dyed sample of the new anti-dissociation drug. To resume, the master propaganda, designed to convince every last individual that the war is crookedly administered, is set to go. Everywhere our agents stand ready to usurp key positions as soon as present civilian executives and war officers gain sufficient insight into the irrationality of their motives as to become incapable of carrying on. You, like the others, have that job to do when, but only when, M'Caslrai and the others—"

"You know, it's a funny thing about M'Caslrai," said Heshifer, stopping dead. "He always reminds me of someone, but I can't think who."

"A living person?" F'Sibr asked patiently.

"No, I don't think so. I almost get it—and then it's gone. You know, we've never really understood M'Caslrai. We've never gotten a convincing line on his phobias or the general form of his delusions. We cannot even classify his psychosis with any confidence. Compared to the others, his mind's a dark book."

"True. To continue, you'll have your job, and a very important one, when M'Caslrai and J'Wilobe and the others lose their grip. Just as I'll have my job, and J'Quilvens hers. There is no justification for endangering the total plan by psychological guerrilla tactics and unnecessary risk-running. J'Quilvens, I disapprove of your bringing that boy here." He nodded toward an archway flanked by bowls of flowers.

"There was no other place."

"That is hardly accurate."

"But he did us a service. Besides, he's gotten his death notice, and we'll need every agent we can get in the war forces. He's obvious officer material—and a teletaction expert. You'll need an aide you can trust, and he might fill the bill."

"Conceivably. Nevertheless, I disapprove of the risk you ran in bringing him here."

"Look, F'Sibr," said Heshifer, his eyes twinkling. "Are you getting a leadership complex?"

"Of course I am. Doubtless if I were a glorified mental sniper, I too could maintain a charming irresponsibility." And F'Sibr grinned, every whit as delightedly as Heshifer. But only for a moment. "To conclude, reports indicate that our plan is proceeding according to schedule. Premature assaults, however appealing, might wreck it."

Heshifer sighed. "It's such a good plan," he said wistfully.

"Well?"

"I was thinking of all the past wars and our counter-plans. They were such good plans too."

"On the contrary, they failed because they contained major flaws. Our present plan is well-calculated."

"The others seemed well-calculated too," said Heshifer softly. "I don't mean to be pessimistic, but I'm the sort of person who doesn't really begin to worry about anything until it threatens his friends—I'd hate to see you two snuffed out along with the rest of the war forces, just because we had such a good plan." Abruptly he grinned. "Look, F'Sibr, I'm worried. Let's get ready—merely get ready—the Chaos Plan, in case."

"The Chaos Plan is worse than no plan at all." F'Sibr's voice had grown gentler than ever, but his face was that of a carven god.

"I don't think so."

"It and the present plan are incompatible. The one would ruin the other."

Heshifer's beard bobbed. "Agreed. But I'm not asking that we put the Chaos Plan into effect—only that we transmit the necessary knowledge to all agents, so they'll be able to use it if the necessity should arise. I have the information in my dossiers on key personnel here and at the Deep Mental Lab."

"The information alone would be too much of a temptation. It could only be imparted with the strict injunction that it never be used except on order from above, and even then we couldn't be sure. I am against it."

THE WOLF PACK

"But I'm worried. Ever since that conference with M'Caslrai and J'Wilobe, I've had the feeling . . . " Heshifer paused and glanced around uneasily.

For once F'Sibr's voice was sharp. "Are you sure that you weren't followed?"

Heshifer didn't reply.

CHAPTER VII

Norm was getting uneasy. Alone in this gray little room it was all too easy to wonder whether this wasn't insanity, rather than what he'd left. The outside world was getting in its licks.

It was hard to keep M'Caslrai's face out of his mind. Like the mask of a guilty conscience, that gaunt solemn visage kept trying to peer over his shoulder, sorrow rather than anger in the dark-circled eyes.

When he thought of his father and mother, of Allisoun, even of Willisoun, the sense of nauseous abnormality, recently so keen, was blunted. He pictured them doing the familiar, inconsequential things that make up the round of daily life.

They were his people. They were home.

Whereas these strangers—

If he'd listened to M'Caslrai—

Perhaps he'd make a big mistake—

He didn't exactly ask himself these questions, but it was becoming hard not to.

He wished J'Quilvens would return. He walked over to the archway, simultaneously becoming aware of a flowery odor that registered unpleasantly—why, he couldn't for the moment remember.

It occurred to him that her "Wait here" hardly constituted an order. Almost before he realized it, he was tiptoeing down the curving corridor.

With every step the odor of flowers became more pronounced.

A little later he saw the source—a room thick as a garden with blooms, each one pouring into the air its sickening stench.

He took a couple more silent steps. He made out among the flowers the amber sleeve of the cryptic fellow who had summoned J'Quilvens. He became aware of a mumble of talk and thought he recognized her voice.

He began to feel embarrassed. He couldn't hear what they were saying, but he knew his actions would be interpreted as those of an eavesdropper—and a silly eavesdropper at that.

41

THE WOLF PACK

Yet to tiptoe back would be sillier still.

Nevertheless, he had about decided to, when something caught his eye.

It was a blue flower in the bowl to the right-hand side of the archway ahead.

One of its petals was rolling and unrolling, like a tiny scroll.

The horror of this tiny action was not diminished by his dreamlike conviction that it was familiar—something he had witnessed a hundred times.

Unwillingly, helplessly, as in a dream, one hand outstretched, he stole forward.

Like trivial detail at the edge of an absorbing picture, the amber-coated man came into view, and beyond him J'Quilvens and a small gnomish person with a white beard.

The petal jerked from the flower, fluttered down, came to rest beside an odd irregularity in the flooring—a double depression like that made by a pair of moccasins.

Another petal began to roll and unroll.

The mumble of talk stopped.

He reached for the flower and his hand encountered in the air a cold, flexible, metallic surface.

There was a whirl of movement. Something slammed into his shoulder. The block in his mind lifted. He remembered who always fingered flowers.

Half reflex, half calculation—his hands grabbed at the air and closed on a metal-sleeved forearm. There was a jerk and he rocked forward. From where the forearm's hand would be, a dazzling blue beam hissed past his face, scorching his cheek. Twisting away, he shifted his grip, one hand sliding toward the wrist, the other twining, getting leverage.

There was a spatter of molten drops as the blue beam traveled along the ceiling into the room ahead, and down. He was dimly aware of figures diving to either side.

There was a smothered grunt of pain. The blue beam was extinguished and something hit the floor with a tiny thud. The pinioned arm writhed free of his grip. Two bowls of flowers crashed to the floor a dozen feet ahead.

Then everything froze. As if they were parts of a scene revealed by a lightning flash, Norm noted the smoldering path of the beam, the scattered flowers, J'Quilvens crouched beyond them, the gnome-like old man peering over an upset table, the amber-coated man on hands and knees but starting up, like a leopard about to spring. In the whole room, nothing moved, save the eyes of those three.

Where the tiny thud had come from, Norm noted a faint depression in the flooring, as if a lightweight object rested there.

Something crushed one of the scattered flowers.

The old man popped up, arm raised and threw. A small jar shattered in the air a few feet from Norm, loosing a splash of red dust.

A partial man of red dust darted toward Norm. He recoiled.

The amber-coated man sprang.

Red dust and amber coat tangled, slammed down near the faint depression.

The blue beam flared again, charred a crazy design on the ceiling, came down, shortened to inches, splashed molten sparks from fading red dust, scared something else.

There was a muffled scream of agony. The beam continued to flare for several more seconds.

Then Norm realized the amber-coated man was getting to his feet, that the old man was fumbling near a smoking hole in the dust-freighted air eight inches off the floor, that J'Quilvens was watching.

The amber-coated man was looking at him coolly, and he heard him say, "I think you were right about the boy, J'Quilvens."

He heard the old man remark pedantically, "Now that's an interesting reflection on scientific progress. Here we have a complete electronic warning system, and this invisible fellow slips right through because every radiant impulse is neatly routed around him. Whereas any primitive alarm system set off by the weight of a passing person would have shown him up instantly. Though that too would have failed if he had combined levitation with invisibility. But if we had a sure, simple way of detecting air displacement . . . "

He pulled something away, and after a brief scrutiny rolled it back. Willisoun's dead face was not pleasant.

"Useful, this fabric," he commented. "Though fortunately not strong enough to reroute a burn blast. J'Wilobe must have some research projects we don't know about. Bad. We'll want to analyze this stuff carefully."

"Yes," said the amber-coated man sharply. "But not now, and not here." J'Quilvens and the old man looked around.

"We have only minutes," he told them. "Maybe they didn't have a spy-beam tracing Willisoun—or another invisible man!—but you can bet their instruments picked up that burn blast. And how long does it usually take J'Wilobe's men to draw a cordon in the Old City? Come on!"

The amber-clad man looked exactly like a wolf then, and Heshifer like an old wolf, well exercised, and J'Quilvens like a pliant wolf girl.

CHAPTER VIII

Like a dark star traveling toward collision with Earth, hurtling or barely crawling across the interstellar void according to which time-scale nervous minds chose, the war entered its fifth month.

From thousands of noiseless, nerve-wrackingly unreal factories weapons and equipment poured forth. Silently triphibian-sections swung together, interwove, were flawlessly joined. In an unending slow-paced stream the completed transports slid stealthily into the air, bound on test runs outside the atmosphere and in the depths of the ocean on whose restless surface their final destiny would be worked out.

From robot farm and mine, streams of grain and metal flowed to dumps near ports of embarkation. There too went the barges that would carry the materials on the last leg of their journey. People gazed in awe at these gargantuan stockpiles. An ancient war would eat them steadily, day by day, but this war must take them at one gulp.

Civilians went about with surface casualness, working longer, eating skimpier, playing less. The fear that had troubled them on the first night had retreated deep into their nerves, where it did not lack for companions.

Amusement areas were closed, except to those who could show a death notice. Inside them, unlimited pleasure was provided, since a softening as well as a hardening of fiber was part of the plan for the chosen.

Religion, such as it was, thrived. The ministers of the man-worshipping cult did boom-town business. Monster mass-meetings were held daily, with believers either telepresent or in the flesh. At them, emotions were purged almost as effectively as, though less painfully than, by the machines in the dungeons of J'Wilobe's secret police. Afterward a few hysterical women would offer themselves for the volunteer service. Among the gray-clad female officers who swore them in was one whose elfin features and smile contrasted sharply with the acid-lipped masculine visage of the average.

THE WOLF PACK

Crime was no longer in the spotlight. Except for unpublicized hunts for deserters and even more hushed proceedings against violators of the morale-code, police activities were nil.

High-ranking officers of the war-forces, already so worried as to how the men under them would behave that they hardly thought of their own approaching fate, met more frequently to work out exercises in logistics. At one such meeting—fair sample of the rest—a dozen men gathered around a transparent globe on which colored dots and dashes represented triphibian squadrons, barge assemblies, divisions.

The ranking officer rose. "Today's problem presupposes a rendezvous in the South Atlantic at the point indicated. How would you handle it, F'Sibr?" An odd note entered his voice as he mentioned the name. Both he and the others showed a peculiar mingling of uneasiness, attraction, and respect as they listened to the big, remote-eyed man explain how the war forces might best make their final five-day voyage.

At thousands of training centers and in the field, men were oriented for death. They met it in every form and guise. They became inured to the hot windy whine of burn-blast and stab-ray, no matter how near were the misses. They learned to face the robot projectile with their number on it and to trap it in a web of close-range fire no matter with what sentient cleverness it ducked and dodged. In transparent armor they crawled on hands and knees through phosphorescent miles of deadly radioactive dust. They were marooned in bathyspheres on the ocean floor and in space suits beyond the moon, only to be rescued at the last moment. At the word of command they stepped unequipped onto the clouds and were caught a few dozen yards above the ground by diving fliers. In conclaves suggesting those of ancient secret societies they drank down cups of wine, every thousandth one of which was supposedly poisoned. An illusion of invulnerability was built up, along with the habit of absolute obedience. A crammed routine of hardship, pain, pleasure, peril, and glory erased private thoughts almost before they occurred and fostered the feeling that each individual was only a cell in the hand that was fingering the gun, would soon raise it to the temple.

CHAPTER IX

Norm was home on furlough. He sat paying lazy attention to a color tune turned on so low that it was only a shifting of shadowy hues around the teletactor. Allisoun leaned her head on his shoulder. His father and mother sat side by side and gazed proudly at the sleek gray uniform with its insignia of rank.

"Who'd ever have thought four months ago," his father philosophized, "that you'd become an officer."

"Not just an officer," his mother corrected. "An aide."

"That's right, Mother. Say, what do you think of this F'Sibr fellow, Norm?"

"Oh—he's rather quiet."

"Now that's very interesting," observed his father, leaning forward brightly. "Tell me all about your work, Norm. I know it's teletaction, but what exactly do you do?"

"He's tired of talking about that. He wants to enjoy himself. Don't bother him."

"I guess you're right, Mother." But he still regarded Norm hopefully.

Allisoun squeezed Norm's hand gently.

Norm smiled. He was remembering J'Quilvens. Last week they had been alone together, just after he had received a routine hypnotic treatment from F'Sibr to strengthen his mind against government propaganda. He had made love to her. She had threatened to have F'Sibr implant a posthypnotic dislike for her in his mind. And then she had started him talking about his original ideas for communications sabotage.

J'Quilvens was an oddly attractive girl, oddly enticing . . . and oddly remote.

He returned the pressure of Allisoun's hand and put his arm around her.

He didn't admire himself for it, but he had to admit that he enjoyed Allisoun's submissiveness and the way she crawled for favors.

THE WOLF PACK

Just as he took a cruel pleasure in playing up to his parents' admiration of his uniform and egging them on to say ridiculous things—despite his new understanding of them.

It made him feel uneasy and rather disgusted, but he was unable to resist, basking ironically in his pseudoglory.

His father couldn't keep quiet. "It certainly is amazing the way Norm's come along. I'll frankly admit—because I was wrong—that I didn't think he'd make a good soldier. And you'll agree that Norm's behavior, when he first got the news, wasn't encouraging. We were even afraid he'd desert! But now it appears that a military career is the very thing for him. Just goes to show how little we know about people—even our own." He stood up, directing his genial lecture at his wife and Allisoun. "Look how he's succeeded. An officer—an aide, Mother!—in four months! Why there's no telling to what heights he may rise, no limit to the positions he may attain—except, of course, that . . ."

He realized his blunder. The silence became painful. He hurried over to the teletactor and began to fiddle with the controls. Faint colors and sounds came and went.

"Any news of Willisoun?" Norm asked lazily.

His mother answered for Allisoun. "Not a word! He must be off on some very important mission, because Allisoun has inquired again and again at his office, but they won't tell her anything."

"I can't understand why he doesn't 'tact' me," Allisoun murmured.

"It must be a very secret mission, dear," Norm's mother said.

Norm nodded.

"I'm sorry," said Allisoun hesitatingly, "that you and he had that . . . disagreement before he went away."

Norm nodded and smiled.

A tall ghostly figure materialized in front of the teletactor, became solider as his father adjusted the controls. It stood with its feet sunk in the floor because the teletactor was a little off level.

The gaunt suffering face was M'Caslrai's. Norm sat up straighter. His jaw set. Allisoun looked around at him curiously.

" . . . because it has always been my practice to talk frankly to critics and detractors," came the tired, plodding voice. "The so-called neo-humanitarians have made their plea against certain aspects of the war. This is my answer: It is because we do not want to see humanity tortured and degraded by conflict that we do this thing. The conscientious objectors have advanced their claims. But I say to them: Be thankful. You are not asked to kill, only to give your lives. The advocates of a 'token' sacrifice have made their suggestions. But I tell them: You can't fool reality with 'token' payments. You can't appease the death-wish with any such shallow trick. Would that we could, folks! Would that we could!"

Norm clenched his fists and twisted a little, like a small boy being upbraided by his parent. It was insanity that M'Caslrai was mouthing, he reminded himself fiercely. Stark lunacy. And yet . . .

"To all of you I say this: He who casts doubt upon our dreadful sacrifice, he who seeks in the slightest degree to sabotage our war, is a traitor to all . . . "

Norm was on his feet. The others were staring at him astonished.

"Shut it off, will you! Shut it off!"

CHAPTER X

Heshifer let his thoughts ramble. There were so many ways of playing the present situation—of taking advantage of the cumulative death-wish of mankind—that he wished he lived in a dozen worlds so he could try them all. For instance, they could seek to direct the death-wish at an outside enemy, by faking an invasion—not from Mars or Venus anymore, but from one of Jupiter's moons or just the interstellar unknown. But that had been tried seventy-five years ago and it hadn't worked. Or desperate diseases justifying desperate remedies, they might attempt to divide the war forces into two groups that would fight each other. Or, better yet, get them to turn around and to conquer the rest of the world. But that, as bitter experience had shown, was as impossible as telepathy.

Of course, he thought wistfully, there was always the Chaos Plan. Dangerous admittedly, and unpredictable, perhaps even ungovernable. But then, what wasn't? Government was ungovernable! He wished they were at least prepared to employ the Chaos Plan. Fortunately, it was beginning to look as if that necessity might never arise. The Sanity Scheme and the F'Sibr propaganda seemed to be working out. Still, plans were treacherous things. One never knew. F'Sibr trusted so completely in the idea that only society was crazy, that individuals were mainly sane and would recognize their insanity if properly propagandized. An attractive paradox, and possibly true. Well—F'Sibr and Sanity must have their day, but if they failed, then Heshifer and Chaos!

"I often wonder," mused M'Caslrai, looking across the desk, "what you're thinking about, Mister Heshifer, when you get that expression on your face."

As Heshifer took a moment to consider his reply, he wondered for the hundredth time of whom the World Director reminded him.

*

J'Wilobe was lonely. Sometimes he felt horrible sure that of all men, he and he only had the slightest inkling of the myriad murderous conspiracies

50

that were drawing their webs tighter and tighter around the world and him. A circle of malignant intellects, human and alien, surrounded the world and him, sending out tentacles. Their hostile thoughts exerted a tangible pressure. Everywhere you looked, there was evidence. Were the others blind fools, that they could not see? Whom could he really trust? Not even Inscra. Not even M'Caslrai. Of course, those two seemed to have some superficial understanding of the threat to the war, ever since he had demonstrated it so conclusively. M'Caslrai especially. But not even M'Caslrai would permit him to take such obvious steps as arresting Heshifer on suspicion. When it was plain to see, since Willisoun had disappeared while trailing Heshifer, that Heshifer must be in the plot. But M'Caslrai refused to see it, and Heshifer went about his business unchecked. Well, let him! Let the others be blind! He, never more rightfully the Secretary of Dangers than now, had eyes enough for them all. And at least there were no longer any hindrances to his questionings of minor prisoners. When the emotion machines had done with them, when they had laughed and cried and feared and hated until they could no more, then they would talk. Then J'Wilobe would . . .

"I think I know what you're afraid of, Mister J'Wilobe," M'Caslrai said to him, smiling faintly. "But I also think I know how we're going to get around it when the time comes." He waggled his finger, desisting when he saw the expression in J'Wilobe's eyes.

CHAPTER XI

Beneath the surface, things were not going well with the war.

There were whispers. No one could say who started them, hardly even who repeated them. They were like the muttering voices the mind hears when it is drunk with fatigue. But they traveled. They did things.

A riot in an amusement area. A work-stoppage that left uncompleted triphibians roosting helplessly. At a training center, a veiledly mutinous refusal to undergo further death-tests, with the officers mainly intent on concealing the evidence of their own inefficiency. At a government center, open criticism of officials, mass protests, shocking accusations.

The burden of the whispers was always the same: That the war was being crookedly administered. That it had only been decided upon because M'Caslrai's government was tottering. That death notices had gone only to those individuals whose independence and honesty made them a threat to the M'Caslrai regime. That no actual friend of the M'Caslrai regime had been chosen.

Facts and figures were provided to prove this. Individuals were named. Everyone was supplied with a ready-made personal grievance.

There grew a spirit of negativism, of smoldering resentment, of cynical disbelief in the whole fabric of society. There were sly sneers, spasms of sudden rage, guarded questionings of things held most sacred, deadly accusing glances.

Rehabilitation centers for deviants filled, overflowed. The same thing happened to the temporary detention centers and the unpublicized dungeons. Closely guarded orders went out: "Except for ringleaders, no more arrests . . . "

Along with the whispering, half-masked by it, there went more individualized form of psychological sabotage. It was as if, in the midst of a general barrage, a hidden sniper were picking preferred targets with a cold deliberation and slamming into their brains bullets of a far higher speed and greater destructiveness—mental bullets.

Here a morale expert fell foaming with convulsions in the midst of an address, later opened dazed eyes that doubted everything. There a communications specialist began surreptitiously to play with the tape-spools of his trade—pile them up in toy skylons. Elsewhere an actuary was found working out statistically detailed plans for the complete destruction of human life throughout the solar system and the erasing of all signs of its presence.

An empty-eyed officer at a training center recorded for teletaction an announcement beginning: "A token plan has been adopted. Death candidates desiring discharge will report to . . . " Before the announcement was killed, it was seen by dozens. When questioned, the horror-stricken officer could only recall that, just before going to sleep the previous evening, he had seen rhythmically bobbing lights, heard a drowsy insistent voice.

A police official woke in the night and listened in terror and relief to a voice which told him that his crushing sense of guilt was merely due to a submerged memory of the many times he had imagined the death of his father.

A minor executive looked up with drug-filled eyes and asked: "Are we saviors . . . or murderers? Are we . . . sane?"

A billion throats threatened to take up that most dreaded question, until it became a scream heard around the world.

*

Gradually the forces opposing the war drew even with those furthering it, until they teetered in precarious balance.

At Supracenter M'Caslrai rose and surveyed his secretaries. His head was bowed, as if the skull, molding the tired flesh in its image, were made of lead.

"Gentlemen," he said, "a greater strength than ours is needed. We must ask guidance of omniscient, omnipotent Man." There was a murmur of agreement. "Dark teleconclaves for that purpose must immediately be called throughout the world. We here, as well as the rest, must join in supplication, ourselves to ourselves."

Across the round table, Heshifer smiled inwardly. This was a moment he had been waiting for.

At the appointed conclave time, the smile appeared openly on Heshifer's face. Sitting alone in his office in the Deep Mental Lab, he made certain trifling adjustments to a small instrument on his desk. Then he slipped on his telemask.

He erased the smile as the black velvet mouths of the mask settled snugly over his eyes, nose, and lips, swung back and covered his ears. Leisurely he pulled on his telegloves. Thus equipped, he could exercise his senses and manipulate objects through electronic counterpart-hands at any place in the world, or off it, where a teletactive unit existed. He could consult tapes in any library, savor a beverage in Africa, sign his name to a document on the moon, or strangle a man on Mars.

He could function in any properly equipped assembly chamber anywhere.

Or, as would happen now, he could functionally assemble with a hundred others in a chamber no bigger than an egg. In such a dark teleconclave, which in some ways resembled an ancient multiway telephone call, the electronic micro-counterparts of each participant would be brought together at a central point, according to any chosen assembly pattern, and the resultant images faithfully transmitted back to each participant.

Plunged in soothing darkness, though still perfectly aware that he was sitting at his desk, Heshifer waited. Then, like white masks, other faces floated into view. Gradually the assembly pattern became clear—a sphere of closely packed inward-turned faces.

He recognized J'Wilobe, Inscra, and other high executives and supervisors. Automatically his mind ticked off: paranoia, catatonia, melancholia, cosmic shock, dictatoria, ethical monomania, omniscientia, newsman's psychosis, creative paralysis, hypertrophic realism, commissaria, permanent escapism, Manism, negatimania, the Venusioid delusion, and dementia praecox.

Then he saw M'Caslrai, and his mind ticked off a question mark.

The conclave was complete.

Counterpart-hand grasped neighboring counterpart-hand, linking the elements of the sphere.

There was a feeling of primal pulsation, as if they were the inward-peering walls of a life-cell swimming in dark immensity.

Then, like the nucleus of such a cell, something pale and pinkish-sallow began to materialize at the central point toward which all eyes were directed.

A reverently mellow voice spoke, "Oh Man, Manipulator of Destiny, from our trouble we appeal to you." And they all repeated, "Oh Man, hear our voice."

The central mistiness grew denser, became the forms of a man and woman of matchless beauty, an eternal Adam and Eve.

Heshifer, like everyone else, knew that these forms were teletactive projections from taped recordings. Religious doctrine, however, hinted that the forms were influenced by the worshippers' ideals.

"Oh Man, Shaper of Earth and Scaler toward Heaven, give us of your inexhaustible wisdom and strength."

The central couple, heads proudly upheld, smiled faintly and distantly, like gods riding on the clouds. Their flesh glowed with an inward radiance, lighting the faces around them.

"Oh Man, grant our desires."

There was to Heshifer something inexpressibly distasteful about this self-worship, this adulation of the species, this slobbering over the image in the mirror. When the voices chorused, it was like fish mouths opening and shutting around a central bait. He took advantage of the flurry of religious fervor to withdraw one of his hands from the web, maneuvering the hand that gripped it to grip instead two free fingers of his other hand.

THE WOLF PACK

"We have wandered in darkness, because we did not keep your image in our hearts.

"We erred because we forgot you."

A feeling of cozy and ego-inflating security began to enfold the worship cell. Heshifer withdrew his free hand from its teleglove and touched the instrument on his desk.

"You grant us leadership, and we are in danger.

"You gave us the helm and now storms threaten."

But something had begun to happen to the central figures—though the change was so slight that anyone but Heshifer might have thought it merely a trick of the mind. The glorious forms seemed to stoop a little, there was the barest suggestion of a slouch. The faces shortened and bulked out a trifle. Something sullied infinitesimally the radiance of the flesh. Heshifer smiled gently and continued the adjustments.

"Oh Man, Perfectest of All Things, Apex of Evolution's Pyramid, without whom the universe would be only death and dead matter . . ."

Imperceptibly the change was progressing. The two hairlines were creeping downward and a certain sporadic dark downiness had become apparent. The slouch was definite, the hands reached for the knees. The features were pouting together, thrusting forward a little with a petulant air.

"You who are the Breath of all Beauty, Sensitive and Delicate beyond compare . . ."

And now there was a slight change in the leading voice too. It was still mellow and profound, impeccably so, but one fancied irony rather than reverence. Though that too might merely have been a matter of mood.

Moving only his eyes, Heshifer surveyed the inward wall of faces. Some of them looked definitely worried—and trying to conceal it. That was good.

"You who are the Crown of Life, the Priceless Ornament of Existence, matchless in grace . . ."

And now the trend of the change in the two central figures was obvious. The slouch had become a stoop-shouldered slump. Legs had shortened and bowed. Hands had reached knees and seemed inclined to go beyond. The sporadic downiness had become ever thickening hairy patches. More and more obviously it was becoming an ape-man and his bride squatting in darkness, squinting surlily.

Practically every one of the inward-peering faces seemed to be trying to hide worry now. More than worry—disgust and fear. So far as Heshifer could judge, each thought that only he could see the imperfection of the vision—and feared that the imperfection was a mirroring of his own secret and unclean thoughts—and so tried not to show it.

He felt one electronic grasp on his counterpart-hand tighten conclusively, then guiltily slacken.

"Being without Flaw, Paragon of Gentleness and Humility . . . "

The male figure gave its consort a shove, then smirked and thumped its chest. The color of the light had changed. It was becoming reddish, murky, flickering—a wood fire's glow. The surrounding darkness was that of a soot-blackened cave.

"You who have transcended the animals and are above all gross things . . . "

Both figures were now peering downward with great interest, and scratching.

"You whose thoughts trend always heavenward, whose eyes are fixed on the stars . . . "

The male caught something, inspected it minutely, then snapped it between horny fingernails. The female craned her neck curiously.

Heshifer rejoiced. The inward-peering faces looked sick and sweating as they strove to maintain the pretense. Obviously their value-scales were shaking at the foundation. It was working out better than he ever had hoped. He'd never dreamed he'd be able to let it go this far.

But, he noted suddenly, there was an exception. All the faces showed smothered disgust and horror and shame—except one.

THE WOLF PACK

M'Caslrai's dark-ringed eyes were gazing tranquilly at the two ape-creatures with an expression that could only be interpreted as compassion and tenderness. It was as if the spirit behind the gaunt homely face reached out and embraced even these lowly beings, or as if he understood that this too was the nature of man.

The sense of a resemblance to some other and well-known personality was so strong that Heshifer swore that in a moment he'd remember who. But he didn't.

Never had the secret of M'Caslrai's personality seemed so close—or so far.

Heshifer's mood changed abruptly, from one of exulting confidence to gnawing doubt. Somehow, what he saw in M'Caslrai's face took away all his certainty of success.

Abruptly he came to a decision on a matter to which he had not given a thought all day.

F'Sibr or no, he would prepare the Chaos Plan.

CHAPTER XII

It was Embarkation Day. In a score of great harbors around the world, the fleet rode at anchor. The tiny Martian and Venusian contingents had arrived; their opalescently space-weathered hulls stood out from the rest. The robot barges bearing the vast stores were already at sea, waiting.

In each hull, robot-or man-carrying, even in the smallest auxiliary launches and fliers, was a disintegrative core keyed to a master detonator aboard the fleet flag-triphibian Finality.

All was ready, and on the surface all was well. But below the surface . . .

There was mutiny aboard a quarter of the triphibians. It was being temporized with. Elsewhere, mutiny was close to the surface.

Extraordinary rumors were surging about. Perhaps the chief one was that a "token" war plan involving no human deaths was being forced through Supracenter by M'Caslrai himself. Another was that the war forces would be called upon to wipe out rebellious civilians, destroy all the old cities.

Chaplains hurried about, nervously invoking man to remain true to his divine self, calling on him to meet without flinching the supreme enemy Death.

Scattered companies of women's volunteers made hysterical attempts to desert and were forcibly confined to their quarters.

All over the world there was open demand for the dissolution of the M'Caslrai government, the abandonment of the war, and the immediate return home of death notices.

A powerful civilians' committee, organized overnight, had presented Supracenter with an ultimatum.

And Supracenter did not act. It made no move to crush the mounting rebelliousness. It stayed behind locked doors. No one knew what was going on behind those doors, but from the cracks around them a miasma of weakness welled.

Everywhere there was an extraordinary atmosphere of nervous tension. People cringed, as if fearful that each increase of pressure would set off a universal scream. There was a wild, glorious joyfulness at the idea of stopping the war and saving fifty million lives. At the same time there were waves of guilt at the thought of the reckless daring of the course that was being taken, the blasphemous flaunting of a century's profoundest rituals. And there were recurrent gusts of the early irrational fear of an unknown enemy who would swoop down suddenly out of space.

These opposed feelings beat against each other, drove each other higher and higher, toward an inevitable climax.

And still Supracenter did not act.

Spruce in his pearly dress uniform, Norm stood on the dress bridge of the fleet flagphip Finality and looked across the harbor toward the city. Norm had the unnerving feeling that his mind was a sounding board for the confused emotions of humanity—each breath of hope, each blast of guilt. So he tried to keep his mind empty, occupied—not with rehearsing the part he must play in the Fleet Teletaction Room when the crisis came, for he knew that by heart—but with trivial things.

Nature had done her best here to make it a gala Departure Day. One hardly noticed the dark cloudbank to the west. Sunlight glittered on the blue wavelets, shimmered on the silvery hulls of the massed triphibians.

They crowded the harbor, their sleek shapes making them seem like a school of giant silver whales—or the gods of whales.

Tiny, gleamingly uniformed figures thronged the dress bridges, structures which could be retracted for aerial, submarine, or extraterrestrial operations.

Fliers and copters darted about.

Beyond the great silverbacks, the ugly walls of the Old City loomed. But beyond those, dwarfing them, lost in the blue haze, shot up the fairy pinnacles of the New City—midmost the golden shaft of Supracenter, drawing the gaze toward the blinding sky and so back to the bridge in a track paralleling the palisade of storm clouds to the west.

Behind him Norm glimpsed a group hurrying into the Fleet Command Room—Fleet Commander Z'Kafir, Flagphib Commander Sline, and Fleet

Communications Officer F'S:br among them. They exuded an air of portentous secrecy.

He saw J'Quilvens slipping past them in the opposite direction, trim in her Liaison Officer's uniform. He tried to catch her imps' candles of eyes, but failed. He felt a sharp irrational pang of uneasiness and guilt.

Looking toward Supracenter, he noted a silver sliver projecting from its peak; also an increase in the number of clustering fliers. Then his glance wavered as lightning flickered from the approaching storm wall to the west. But his mind did not analyze these impressions.

J'Quilvens had made him think of Allisoun. He pictured her as he'd seen her yesterday—in tears at his departure. Poor kid, he'd treated her rottenly, strutting before her, taking advantage of her hysterical affection, while all the time he didn't care a stick for her.

She had not gloated over their relationship, as he had cynically predicted, gloried in being a doomed man's lover. She hadn't wanted him to die; she'd clung to him.

Of course, there was his feeling toward J'Quilvens, but that only made his behavior toward Allisoun worse.

A fine way for a world-savior to act toward a girl who was only trying to make him happy!

The silver sliver had lengthened a trifle, and the fliers had clustered thicker yet—or else there were other tinier shapes among them. Again lightning flickered, and there came a growl of thunder.

At the very least, he shouldn't have taken such cruel pleasure in her grief, especially when he knew that if all went well he was not going to die. Of course, he couldn't very well have revealed any plans to her, but at least he could have let drop a hint, given her a ray of hope.

And he'd killed her brother, or helped kill him, and then gotten a kick out of her innocent worries over his absence. Willisoun had been a spy and murderer, had deserved to die, but still that didn't justify his own nasty hypocrisy.

THE WOLF PACK

The silver sliver was obviously much longer than it had seemed at first. The fact that it was directed toward the harbor had foreshortened it. And still it lengthened. The tinier shapes seemed to be gathered in tiers around it, and there was a suggestion of movement on the roofs of the Old City. This time the thunder was accompanied by some other solemn rumbling.

It was the same with his parents. They weren't the selfish Philistines he had pictured them; they were just a little scared man and woman trying to do their best in a jumbled world. They hadn't deserved his bitter contempt, to be treated as ridiculous buffoons. He remembered his father's handclasp and choked voice, his mother's sobs.

Whatever the silver sliver was, it was directed like a serpent's neck or the arm of a giant crane, from Supracenter's summit out over the agitated roofs of the Old City. The perplexing aerial tiers seemed to be lengthening with it, flanking it on either side. The rumble had become a steady roll, in which the intermittent western thunder joined. There was a suggestion that the flashes of lightning from the encroaching storm were somehow being answered from the city. There was a hint of martial music, a sudden flurry of movement on the bridges of the farther triphibians.

How could he ever have been so rotten to treat them that way? All of a sudden Norm had the horrible feeling that he was no longer a man cleaving to a dangerous course but a boy caught misbehaving, a juvenile delinquent. He had sneered at his elders, disobeyed, broken the rules, joined a forbidden gang, would be punished. Against all logic, this disgustingly childish fear persisted. He remembered old scenes—times he had rebelled, been "talked to," been forced to recant his boyhood heresies.

A sudden swell in the martial music exploded this dark train of reverie. Like a man waking from a dream, he took his hands from the rail, moved backward a step, looked up.

He knew that something was happening around him, something critical involving the fleet, the city, the world. And yet, like a man still half in a dream, he couldn't comprehend what it was.

The sense of fear crystallized to an icy lump.

FRITZ LEIBER

The silver something arching out from Supracenter was a delicate aerial pontoon bridge, supported by flying components, as it extended itself questingly over the farther triphibians, swaying gently from side to side like a silver serpent's head. There were human figures on it, and the tiers flanking it in the air were made up of human figures too, though how they were supported he couldn't understand. The uniformed mites on the more distant dress bridges were drawing themselves up in ranks. And from the same direction there began to come a steady, frantic cheering, keeping up through the music and the thunderous drumming, building toward a titanic shout.

Z'Kafir, Sline, and the rest of the staff poured suddenly from the Fleet Command Room. He half-expected F'Sibr to address him. But he was brushed by.

There was a running to and fro, a barking of orders. He found himself lining up with the others. He looked around stupidly, realized he was in the first rank.

He saw the women's volunteers lining up, J'Quilvens among them. He heard the flagphib's orchestra join in the general heart-quickening din.

He saw the aerial bridge reaching downward toward the Finality.

And then, at last, he became aware of the whispered word running up and down the ranks. His numbed mind patched together the phrases into the single hope-shattering story.

M'Caslrai and his entire secretariat were joining the fleet. They would share in its destruction. This was their answer to the civilians' ultimatum.

*

Dully he looked at the approaching bridge. Already he thought he could identify some of the figures.

The flanking tiers, he saw now, were teletacted images of people from all over the world, come to witness and applaud Supracenter's sacrifice.

Music, drumroll, and thunder and cheering had now become ear-splitting. Great, unopposable waves of emotion were rolling down from Supracenter across the harbor.

THE WOLF PACK

The black storm wall, grown mountain high, had reached the western shore. Lightning flashes played from it and were answered by the electric guns of the fleet, salvoing salutes. But the aerial bridge was still in bright sunlight, backgrounded by blue.

Norm felt the presence of a giant ghostly figure—Man the God, standing behind the storm wall and peering down over it in divine approval.

A telescoped silver gangplank shot upward from the Finality, linked with the aerial bridge. Slowly the group of figures started down, acknowledging the homage of the world's massed teletacted ranks.

But for Norm the scene drew in. As they came closer, he failed to note that some of M'Caslrai's companions did not share their leader's sad, tranquil satisfaction—that some faces even showed stunned amazement and dry-lipped horror. He had eyes only for one man.

It was as if he and M'Caslrai were alone at the ends of a long but shortening corridor.

This was the man he could not face, the living symbol of paternalistic loving authority down the ages.

His sense of guilt grew beyond all sane proportion. He told himself that M'Caslrai had come to reprimand him, that M'Caslrai would halt before him and with fatherly sternness denounce him as a traitor, that he would be forced to go down on his knees and beg the world's forgiveness.

It was unfair, he protested to himself. M'Caslrai was only a teletacted speechmaker, a signature on world directives, a thought atop Supracenter. He had no right to come down and face you in the flesh.

M'Caslrai stepped onto the bridge. The tumult reached its climax. It seemed to Norm that the big, gaunt man was walking straight toward him. He wanted to run, to plunge through the deck, to be snatched into the sky, to hurl himself at M'Caslrai and strangle him.

He only stood there licking his lips, trembling.

M'Caslrai looked at him once, closely, then passed by.

*

FRITZ LEIBER

At the first possible moment, while the salutes were still thundering the triphibians out of harbor, Heshifer told F'Sibr how the whole maneuver had been engineered by M'Caslrai alone, had come as a complete surprise to practically everyone of the secretariat, himself included.

"And now, the Chaos Plan," he finished.

F'Sibr hesitated, shook his head. "We still have almost a week. Perhaps, all appearances to the contrary, they have played into our hands. Very likely M'Caslrai is contemplating a last-minute escape. But whether he is or not does not matter. We shall see that he escapes—with publicity enough to brand him as a cheat forever. We have the Unseen. It will kidnap M'Caslrai and the other higher-ups, including yourself. It will be handled in such a way as to look like deliberate flight—you will help see to that."

Heshifer frowned.

F'Sibr threw up his hands. "Then, if that fails, you can have your way. The Chaos Plan is ready. It would take only a word."

Heshifer thought. "How many besides the officers of the Unseen will have to be in on the plot?" he asked.

"My aide Norm. Perhaps one or two more."

Heshifer looked up. "You're sure you can depend on him?"

"Absolutely."

After a pause Heshifer nodded unwillingly.

"We have five days," said F'Sibr.

CHAPTER XIII

For three days the fleet had driven across calm seas, slowly, at not a tithe of its real speed, a parade of silver hearses. For three days the death tension had mounted.

The time had come when men began to see visions, hear faint whisperings in the air, feel the touch of currents from beyond life.

Alone on the dress bridge, Norm stared at the sunset. The sun was an arched furnace door on the horizon, the sea a metallic expanse. Astern curved the triphibian battle line, a succession of diminishing silver teardrops, until they were lost in the dusky western blue. Ahead some of the scouts could be seen, fanned out expectantly, as if death might make a premature attack. No sound, save the slightest hiss of displaced waters.

It seemed to Norm that his mind quested over all the sea's brazen plain, without finding a place to rest. There was only the feeling of the grandeur of the fleet, the sense of a proudly onrushing destiny, the suggestion of supernatural wings hovering overhead—and those were the last things he wanted to feel.

He remembered the plan for tonight, but his mind veered quickly.

Perhaps if he sent his mind still farther . . . to the rim . . . beyond . . .

M'Caslrai stood beside him, black elbows on the rail.

Norm's heart jumped, thumped, quieted.

For a while they leaned side by side, watching the sea.

"Maybe a man can find peace out there," said M'Caslrai. "Leastways he can look for it."

A pause. "We're all looking for peace, Mister Norm."

Another pause. Then softly, "You've a girl back there, you told me. What did you say she was called?"

He repeated "Allisoun" thoughtfully after Norm. "And there'll be a child? He will bear your name, I suppose, if a boy. Well, Man willing, he will not have to suffer what you suffer. We may hope that your sacrifice will bear fruit, that in the future the world will take the course of wisdom."

He turned his sorrowful tranquil eyes on Norm. "I feel very small and very troubled," he said. "It is not easy to bow to necessity, to see the few doomed for the sake of the many."

Norm started to speak, mumbled an unintelligible word.

"I'm glad I'm going with you," said M'Caslrai.

The moment passed, was lost with the last blinding sliver of sun. Gloom raced across the sea.

"Tell me, Mister Norm," M'Caslrai asked, "are you troubled?"

Norm hesitated, shook his head.

M'Caslrai nodded, smiled, moved away.

For a moment Norm's mind was numb. Then loneliness rushed in, as if he and M'Caslrai were the only two beings in the world and had parted forever.

He felt giddy, as if the sea were suddenly tilting, as if all his intentions and beliefs were swinging on the bob of a gigantic pendulum.

He looked along the rail to where, unapproachable now, the World Director still stared over the sea.

It's true, he thought. I've always run away from him. All my attitudes have been shaped by fear that, if I ever listened to him, he would persuade me.

It's unfair, something childish inside him reiterated bitterly. He has no right to come down from his pedestal and meet you face to face like an ordinary man. If only he wouldn't, it would be so easy to be true to the others.

But he has come down, the adult reminded. And now there are certain thoughts that you must think, even though each one sears your ego like a red-hot iron.

He is great and wise and compassionate. You can see it in his face, hear it in every word he utters.

He thinks only of mankind, and of what must be, if mankind is to go on.

THE WOLF PACK

Whereas you and the others, even F'Sibr and Heshifer, are selfish and petty, thinking only of criticism and trouble-making and cynical jibing. You seek to sabotage the great current of history which he guides.

You are crackpot dreamers, one more lunatic fringe trying to pretend that what is, is not. He is a realist. He is right and what he does is right.

The world has always been a horrible place and has exacted horrible sacrifices of humanity. Sanity consists in recognizing the necessity of those sacrifices. He is the sane one.

Faces floated before Norm in the gleaming dusk. Faces he knew. Only now F'Sibr looked like a cruel Eastern god, a paranoid who thought he could change the course of history by his personal fiat; Heshifer, a senile mischief-maker, mouth and mind a-twitch with fantastic schemes or brutal jests; J'Quilvens, a hysteric trembling on the verge of laughter or screams. Behind them, a pale-faced horde of deviants and discontents. For a moment they all leered at him, snickered. Then they wavered, faded, and were blotted out by the visage of M'Caslrai—profound-eyed, understanding, earthy but rising above it, gaunt and homely, infinitely kind.

All Norm's confused and often-denied religious impulses urged, "He is the One. He is Man!"

He felt the mighty presence of the fleet, the comradeship of the millions marked and trained for death. Through the silver hulls and the dusk and the faint hiss of the waves, that comradeship tugged at and captured his heart.

Feeling that his whole life had only been a preparation for this moment, he turned and followed the rail.

"Sir," he began.

M'Caslrai's "Yes?" was the friendliest of whispers.

"There is a grave threat to the safety of the fleet and the success of the whole expedition."

M'Caslrai nodded wearily, as if he had known all along. His gaze did not leave the sea.

Norm swallowed. He said, "Before I go on, I want your promise that those I betray will not be killed or hurt, only held where they can do no harm until it's all over. Also, I do not want my part in this to become known."

M'Caslrai looked at him. "You have my promise, Mister Norm," he said.

Later that night all the searchbeams of the Finality flared out suddenly. For a quarter mile around the flagphib it was bright as day. For yards below the water was milky green.

At first nothing was seen except the towering blunt muzzle of the triphibian next in line.

Then a fine white cloud shot out from the flagphib. It vanished swiftly, but left in its wake a small, bone-white ship grappled to the dress bridge, with a number of similarly white figures swarming aboard the Finality.

An order was shouted. The figures hesitated. Some of them turned back.

A blue flicker of small-arms fire cut them down. The ports of the ghost ship were slammed, and in a rainstorm of blue rays it dove like a frightened fish.

Light and explosions pursued it, sending the emerald water in great chunks.

Rocket-tubes blasting, it shot up suddenly into the air, frantically twisting and turning.

The big beams of the Finality caught it. The hull glowed red . . . white . . .

Spinning out of control, it fell like a meteor. There was a great hiss as the Unseen plunged for a last time into the sea.

CHAPTER XIV

Late the next night Norm stood for a third time on the dress bridge. No lights betrayed the hissing triphibians. They went stealthily as murderers. And yet he sensed the mighty hulls, the millions of sleepless souls cramming them, the incalculably numerous robot barges, all converging on the dawn rendezvous.

But they no longer awakened thoughts of a proud destiny. He could only think of the cylindrical cores and of the disintegratives that packed them.

The sharp sense of reality and duty that had inspired him last night was gone. The sense of guilt that had lifted after his confessions had returned intensified. He remembered the white-hot plunge of the Unseen, the hiss of steam. His emotions were frozen, but not numbed. The night might have been black ice encasing him.

That afternoon a sailor had jumped overboard. A watchful dinghy had recovered him, although he had done his best to drown. Later he had pleaded to be killed at once and spared the waiting for tomorrow.

Now Norm kept seeing his frantic, babbling face.

He wondered if he should not have insisted on being imprisoned with F'Sibr and the rest, without revealing that he was the informer.

But he knew he could not have kept the secret in then presence, or endured their reproaches when he confessed.

Well, at any rate, M'Caslrai had kept faith. There was something incredibly honest and noble about the man, something that still bound Norm to him by cords of awe, although in all other respects he had come to regret his action so bitterly that he dared not think about it.

If only he could go back . . . But it was too late now to do anything. The kidnap ship was destroyed.

Of course, he could make some wild effort. There were still the subordinate agents on the other ships. He could . . .

But a complete paralysis of will power held him helpless. He knew, for example, that in the War Room behind him was the master switch which would disintegrate the fleet at dawn. But if it had been just at his elbow, and if a child had been pressing it down, he could have done nothing to stop it.

Like some guilt-tortured prophet of olden times, he stared into the darkness, looking for a sign.

CHAPTER XV

In the utter blackness of the brig, though in the gibberish of code-speech, F'Sibr said calmly, "No, I am the one to blame, if we have to talk about blame. I stubbornly persisted when it was obvious that our whole counterprogram had failed. I clutched at the straw of the kidnap plot. And I trusted Normsi."

"That's not your fault," interjected J'Quilvens, "I was the one who introduced Normsi in the first place."

"Irrelevant. The point is . . . "

"Two thirty," came the toneless voice of an agent named Wavel, who possessed the best sense of time among them.

"The point is," F'Sibr continued, "that I trusted Normsi, even when Heshifer had doubts. It was an unforgiveable executive error."

"But when it comes to that, we aren't absolutely sure that it was Normsi who betrayed us," J'Quilvens urged doubtfully.

"The probabilities all lie in that direction."

"For that matter, we cannot even be sure that the kidnap plot has failed."

F'Sibr did not trouble to answer. They could hear the coded whispers of the two agents conversing at the other end of the brig.

"There must be something we can do," said J'Quilvens.

"Yes," said F'Sibr. "We could have adopted the Chaos Plan four days ago. Unfortunately, my opinion carried too much weight." He paused, as if expecting a comment from Heshifer. When none came, he continued, "True, the plan is fully prepared, but all agents are under the strictest orders to wait for word from above."

"But don't you think some of them will go ahead with it, against orders, at the last minute. Unless they've all been unmasked too?"

"That is unlikely. Normsi was acquainted only with those of us who are here—a fact which incidentally constitutes further evidence against him."

"It's odd, in that case," mused J'Quilvens, "that we haven't been asked to reveal the identity of the agents on the other ships—given a taste of J'Wilobe's persuasion. They must know there are more than us."

"It is odd," agreed F'Sibr. "There was something peculiar about the whole business of our being caught—I mean, the way it was done. I sense M'Caslrai's touch, rather than J'Wilobe's, although it's outside M'Caslrai's line."

"Right!" Heshifer's unexpected comment sounded as if he were following a very different line of thought, which the conversation had only chanced to intersect.

When he said nothing more, J'Quilvens pressed, "But granting the others are free, mayn't they go ahead with the Chaos Plan?"

"Yes, but it won't do any good. The fleet explosives are all keyed to the master switch aboard the Finality. Every smallest unit of the fleet, down to the dinghies, is cored with explosives which it would take hours, in some case days, to remove or unkey. At the time of detonation, the water itself will be deadly for leagues around. Everything hinged on our seizing control of the Finality and preventing the master switch from being thrown. Without that, minor successes are futile."

"Then there's nothing we can do?"

"Well . . . I am trying to think of something, as we all are."

"Of course. But you don't think much of our chances?"

Again F'Sibr did not reply.

When J'Quilvens next spoke, she seemed to be trying to push back the darkness. "Then, to keep up our spirits, we have only the hope that when the next war comes, our survivors will be wiser, will forge a sounder counterprogram?"

"No!" said F'Sibr. For once his voice was sharp, though still even and well-modulated. "We do not have that hope. It would be childish to assume so. It has become clear that the world's insanity has reached its crisis. If we had adopted the Chaos Plan, we might have been able to make use of that crisis—the crisis a gun, the Chaos Plan a trigger. But we failed.

THE WOLF PACK

The moment will not come again. After the crisis, the slow mental degeneration sets in. When the next war comes, our weakened organization will adopt an even more futile and unrealistic program. The war will be greater, as the often-indulged death-wish intensifies. It is to such a future that we must calmly look ahead, if we are to behave as realistic adults. Any other future is as impossible as . . . " He chuckled icily as he invoked Heshifer's favorite comparison, " . . . as telepathy."

A shiver seemed to go through the darkness. It infected J'Quilvens' voice. "And yet, you continue to speak in code? Why do you do that, if you know that everything's hopeless?"

"There is such a thing as honoring a lost cause."

This time there was no doubting the shiver. Then cutting across it, came Heshifer's excited words.

"We must contact Normsi!"

The anticlimax provided by this ridiculous statement was so great that J'Quilvens had to choke back hysterical laughter.

"We know the boy," Heshifer sped on. "We know he's no planted traitor. He must have been subjected to extraordinary psychological pressure—and through M'Caslrai. He's a cyclic type. By now, surely, he's regretting it . . . wavering . . . waiting for a push."

F'Sibr's reply was ominously gentle, almost soothing. "I'll grant you there is a chance that Norm's behavior has followed some such course. Though in that case the probability is that he is under as close guard as ourselves and in no position to do anything even if he does have a change of heart. But . . . " His voice became doubly cautious " . . . You spoke of contacting him? I don't quite see . . . "

"Right!" replied Heshifer, so eagerly, so enthusiastically even, that you couldn't help visualizing his grinning, grimacing face, his darting eyes. "Like you, I have been thinking—about how to contact Normsi. I have eliminated all reasonable possibilities, except one—the most unlikely. Something that we have no evidence for, although we have looked for it for decades. But since, no matter how unlikely, it is the only reasonable possibility, we must, if we are logical, employ it. Telepathy."

There was a pause. "Are you forgetting, 'as impossible as telepathy'?" said F'Sibr. "We might as well try black magic."

"Call it the least impossible of the impossibilities, then! Remember, telepathy may depend on the electrical potential of the nervous system. Think of how great the potential must be at a moment like this. Suppose that our receiver, Normsi, is wavering . . . his mind a blank. Call it anything you like! Call it my last foolish tribute to a lost cause! I, at any rate, shall try."

"And I," said F'Sibr softly after a moment. He was echoed.

Suddenly Heshifer laughed—a rich unlikely laugh.

"Excuse me," he said. "But I just happened to realize of whom M'Caslrai reminds me. It is astounding I never thought of it before. It explains the nature of M'Caslrai's insanity, too. It's not who he is, but who he thinks he is. If I'd only realized it before! What I couldn't have done with the man! I've been blind as a bat . . . "

"Two forty-five," said Wavel.

CHAPTER XVI

J'Wilobe sat alone before the executive panel in the Flagship Security Room next to the brig. His face was more pinched than ever. His jewel-bright eyes kept looking from side to side. An hour ago he had dismissed all the guards and multiply locked the door behind them, and the doors of the two vestibules as well. He had become suspicious. True, he had always trusted the guards before, but now the universe had become a shadow world populated by slinking plotters, and he the lone sentry on the wall.

Of course, as he logically recognized, such a situation couldn't go on indefinitely. But he only had to hold out until dawn, and then he would be relieved forever from his crushing burdens. Unless there were another life . . . But that would be too horrible.

He frowned at the massive circular door of the brig, and decided once and for all that he no longer trusted M'Caslrai. Why had M'Caslrai refused to let him eliminate these danger-mongers, at least question them? Why had he refused to tell him the reasons for their arrest when it was obviously a matter for the Secretariat of Dangers? Even the warning about a possible attack by an invisible ship hadn't come until a few minutes before the occurrence.

Of course he had advised M'Caslrai to arrest Heshifer months ago, had warned him against F'Sibr. But that couldn't be the reason, because M'Caslrai had ignored his proposals.

No, the World Director must have some private source of information. Either he had organized an inner spy-system, or had suborned some of J'Wilobe's own men, or was protecting an informer.

Well, at all events, no one but J'Wilobe knew the present combination to the door of the brig, and he could destroy all life inside it at the touch of a finger. Whatever risky or even traitorous course M'Caslrai might be taking, those in the brig were out of the picture.

At the thought J'Wilobe felt a rush of self-confidence, so exhilarating and intense that he sat there trembling. He suddenly knew that whatever threat arose tonight he would be equal to it. It was as if a cloak of invulnerability had been dropped around his shoulders, masking even his one great hidden weakness—the one he dared not even think about, let alone give an outsider a chance of guessing.

There would be threats tonight, yes—he was curiously sure of that—but he would master them.

He looked around the Security Room. It was as neat and metallic as his mind.

He was immune to assault. No one could even telecontact the room or the inner vestibule, except from the fortified outer vestibule.

The panel before him would inform him of any movements in the restricted areas of the Finality. But J'Wilobe had the illusion of a strange clairvoyant extension of his senses that made the panel seem ridiculously crude by comparison. He felt he could sense at once the slightest hostile movement anywhere aboard the ship, throughout the world—even respond to the faintest inimical scratching on the skin of the space-time cosmos.

A light glowed violet, indicating that someone had entered the outer vestibule.

To J'Wilobe it was as if a long-awaited chess-game had begun. Someone had moved pawn to king's fourth.

He instantly whipped on his telemask and was functionally present in the outer vestibule. His hand-counterparts closed on sidearms conveniently present there.

At first glance there seemed to be no one. Suspecting an invisible man, he prepared to crisscross the walls with fire.

Then he saw a hand on the table.

Someone had made an impossible move with a knight.

Just a gloved hand.

Or was it merely a glove, retaining the shape of the hand that had dropped it?

No, it moved. The fingers drummed—or was the hand starting to walk?

It made a fist. Then the forefinger pointed—first away, then swinging it toward him.

Conscious of a greater pang of terror than he had ever known in his life, J'Wilobe found himself back in the Security Room. It spoke well for his courage that moments later, just as the blue light glowed, he was projecting himself into the inner vestibule.

The hand was there. Without hesitating, he directed a needle beam at it. The hand writhed at the touch of the fiery ray, seemed to crumple, then jerked aside—and pointed at him.

Someone had sacrificed a knight.

By a supreme effort of will, he managed for a moment to continue his fire. The hand recoiled, but kept pointing.

Back in the Security Room, he found the hand ahead of him. He tried to pick up a sidearm, but his fingers could not grasp. He lunged toward the control that would flick death through the brig.

But the pointing hand waggled a little, as if to say "No."

The hand looked hurt. Three fingers dangled. They seemed to be crushed.

Perhaps the waggling was only a wounded shaking. But it continued.

J'Wilobe dropped back from the death control.

Someone had played, "Queen takes pawn. Check."

The hand pointed commandingly toward the door of the brig.

J'Wilobe was not conscious of the sting of the sweat running down into his eyes—only that the blur it produced was insufficient to dissolve the hand.

He took a step toward the door.

A part of his mind had analyzed what had happened. The hand was a tele-counterpart, projected by someone who knew his hidden weakness. From the outer vestibule it had re-projected itself to the inner, and so to the Security Room. Now it was only the projection of a projection of a projection. Yet he had badly maimed the original—the impact of the ray had been transmitted.

But that part of his mind had not power over his actions. It was getting farther and farther away from his consciousness, like something fading toward the most distant star.

There was only enough room in his mind for the hand and the combination to the brig, and the former was pushing out the latter.

As he moved step by step toward the door, the moving finger seemed to press on his skull. Now it was a hand of steel, now of marble, now of fleshless bone, now of boneless flesh, now a man's, now a woman's, now M'Caslrai's, now Inscra's, now Heshifer's, now the fingers were serpents' heads with flickering tongues, now they were the red tongues themselves, now the forefinger was a crooked gun pointed at him, now a crushed but inching caterpillar, now a comet zigzagging toward him through blackness . . . eventually all these faded and it became his father's hand, approaching to tickle him, apparently loving, actually cruel. Mind-destroying laughter twitched at his lips.

Checkmate!

The door opened, the finger poked through his skull, the laughter exploded . . . and then the whole world blacked out, and J'Wilobe realized that he had fallen millions of miles and landed in a cozy, velvet-lined cell where he could eternally play a thousand simultaneous blindfold chess games and win them all. With a calm happiness that he had never known before, he made his thousand first moves.

CHAPTER XVII

From the stratospheric heights in which his flier idled, Airscout Mardel overlooked the entire curved area of sea constituting the rendezvous. Rank after rank of triphibian and barge, spaced with geometrical precision except for the few lines of late arrivers. Albino soldier ants on a dark field.

Airscout Mardel's features were the set, hopeless ones of a man who must meet an unvanquishable foe. Even if he had been the sort to consider desertion in battle, he knew that it was doubtful whether there was time enough left for the fastest flight to carry him beyond range of the general blast. And granting he escaped the general blast, there was the disintegrative charge buried in his flier—a relatively small one, but ample for its purpose. Moreover, there would be the other fliers to reckon with. And then there was that omnipresent feeling of an unseen, unknown enemy who would surely engulf any man who straggled far.

The sky had been lightening for some time. Now a blinding chunk of sun shoved above the horizon. It occurred to Airscout Mardel that this was a sunrise which those below would not be privileged to watch.

He looked down again and frowned. He fancied there was a slight jumbling of the ships, a disorder in the ranks, the barest suggestion of a scattering. As if an invisible giant had thrust a stick toward the silver ants.

The commander of the Enterprise looked around the Command Room. He was a florid, portly man. A glance at the panel showed him that everyone was at battle stations, ready for the event. The communications officer gave him a message. The commander read it twice. He began to laugh, softly at first, then in more and more joyful peals. The others edged away. He dropped the message and began to strip off his clothes. The navigation officer picked up the message and read, "The time has come for you to reveal yourself. The sign has appeared—the bloody star. Drop the mask. Speak!" He looked up uncomprehendingly. Naked, the captain strode out onto the dress bridge, crying, "I am Man! I am Man!" A bit of red glowed beside the doorway—it looked like a star-shaped jewel.

Perhaps the communications officer had dropped it—he had come in that way. And now the communications officer was giving orders in a crisp voice.

Aboard the Decision order was given to gather in the mess room for religious service. Almost immediately it was followed by an order to return to battle stations. Then the first order was repeated. Then the second. Again the first. Again the second. When the scrambling was at its most frantic, the executive officer turned up suddenly with a glowing knife and ran through the ship, slashing right and left.

Throughout the fleet, key men screamed at shadows, pawed at phantoms, smirked at the invisible. They listened to nonsensical messages whispered over teletactors and their limbs grew hysterically rigid. They glanced at a foolish picture and went blind. They were shown meaningless bric-a-brac and fell into convulsions. They closeted themselves briefly with teletactive messengers and came out unharmed—in body.

Panic was awakened in subordinates. Each man was a fuse exploding those below him. The thing was contagious, though here and there an oddly cool-headed few sought to stem the confusion—but only after it reached a peak.

The crew of the Mortality abandoned ship. Hundreds of men simply dropped overboard and swam away. Of the four officers who stayed in the control room, one was laughing, another cried, the third crouched horrified in a corner, the fourth was sunk in apathy. They were looking at something that dangled from the control panel.

There was fighting aboard the Remote. Just small arms, until someone ordered the big guns backfired to clear out the corridors. There was a giant flash and a shock wave that smashed a valley in the water. Then there were only the Remote's neighbors heaving on a giant swell caked with silver dust.

The Ultimate turned her guns on the Infinity, disintegrated her, then committed suicide.

THE WOLF PACK

The commander of the Immortality saw something through the forward telescopes. What it was he would tell no one, but he ordered the forward guns fired into the western darkness and the ship itself sent full-speed ahead in pursuit. No one understood, but he was obeyed. He manifested extraordinary excitement as they blasted first into the air and then into outer space. Perhaps it was Death itself he thought he was attacking, for he muttered such things as, "That hurt him, boys! Look, he runs! But we'll track him down even if he lairs on Uranus! Watch out!—he's raised his sting!" He clung to the telescopes. The Immortality blasted away from the sun, toward the outer planets.

There was wild music aboard the Farewell. Red-daubed women and green-smeared men were dancing. Food was strewn, liquors sloshed. The drug lockers had been broken open. Someone had dragged out an emotion machine and was experimenting fantastically.

Aboard the Nightfall they prayed.

✲

It was an hour when minds were jerked open like long-locked drawers and their dark contents blindly strewn. Secret ideas fumed like smoke, obscuring the face of reality. It was not the actual sky and sea, but a delirium of water and air. The paling stars were a paranoid's dream of grandeur. Only insanity was real.

In the Fleet Command Room of the Finality, Commander Sline had collapsed, but Fleet Commander Z'Kafir had the situation well in hand. His mind was clear and cool. He realized what had happened and saw exactly what must be done. But he was speaking at ten times his normal rate, and when he tried to indicate by gestures what must be done, his hands moved too fast to follow. This purely mechanical defect in his ability to communicate rendered all his brilliant ideas useless.

General Secretary Inscra took over smoothly, although he was bothered by the disappearance of M'Caslrai. Phlegmatically he began to give the orders that were locked inside Z'Kafir, when Communications Officer

F'Sibr entered the room. Inscra observed that it was only a teletactive counterpart, but he deduced that F'Sibr was operating from the Fleet Communications Room, and he knew how that room could be destroyed. He made a movement, but F'Sibr opened his hand and extended it toward Inscra.

Inscra's eyes—the eyes which had always seemed the only live things in a dummy figure—now died too.

On the outstretched palm was a large gray spider.

Somewhere the word started and went from ship to ship, first a whisper, then a shout growing toward a cheer. "The war's over!" And then a strange comment was added. "We've won! We've won!"

Cold sweat trickled down Airscout Mardel's forehead. An incredulous joy twisted his tight features. The sun was above the horizon. It drenched the whole sea with gold. It glittered from every last vessel. The moment of disintegration had come and gone—a half-hour ago.

The giant's stick had poked. The silver ants were scattering. Two collided as he watched. Silvery splotches marked the grave of the Remote, the Infinity, and the Ultimate. There was no order or intelligence left.

Airscout Mardel grinned, snarled, "I'm alive!" and sent his flier rocketing crazily toward outer space.

Heshifer darted from the Fleet Communications Room. Never had he seemed quite so old, or quite so active. He was followed by J'Quilvens and Norm, the latter with his right hand cased in transparent plastic where J'Wilobe's needle ray had mangled it.

"We sealed off the War Room at the start," Heshifer explained. "Now we'll draw the fangs of the whole setup."

Perhaps in automatic response to the word echoing through the fleet, Norm murmured to J'Quilvens as they hurried along after, "We've won."

J'Quilvens giggled. "Not by a long sight. We've only driven the fleet crazy. And we'll drive the whole world crazy before we're through. From now on, we're attendants in the violent ward. But it's a beginning—a chance!"

The guards before the War Room stepped aside. Heshifer opened the door—and instantly stopped dead. He motioned everyone to stay where they were. "Above all," he whispered, "don't make a move with your weapons."

Over Heshifer's shoulder, framed by the square of the doorway, Norm could see M'Caslrai. He was standing behind a table that resembled an altar. In it a black rod was vertically set. M'Caslrai looked sad and resolute. The way he stared at them was reminiscent of a sleepwalker. Slowly he began to bear down on the lever.

"Mister President," Heshifer called softly.

M'Caslrai paused. "How did you know the name of my real office?" he asked. "I've been careful to keep that a secret from everyone."

"Mr. President," Heshifer said, "the British ambassador wants an audience. There is an important memorandum from General Scott. And Secretary Seward's here to see you. It's very urgent."

"I know," said M'Caslrai. "I'll be right there. But there's something I must do first." Again he bore down on the lever.

"But there's no time, Mister President," Heshifer interjected. "It's come at last. They've fired on Fort Sumter!"

M'Caslrai's hand fell away from the lever. "So," he murmured softly. "Well, what must be must be." He came around the table and started toward the door. He smiled, almost sheepishly, at Heshifer. "It's a funny thing, Mister Nicolay," he said, "but I was having the darnedest dream—it seemed to last a lifetime. I dreamed they'd made me boss in another world, and there was another war, and there was something I had to do. I wonder . . . "

Then he looked ahead, and his face grew grave and prophetic, as if he were thinking of the brave, bitter times ahead, and the part he must play in them. As he shuffled past, Heshifer heard him mutter as if he were rehearsing that part, " . . . that these dead shall not have died in vain—that this nation, under God, shall have a new birth of freedom—and that government of the people, by the people, for the people, shall not perish from the earth."

www.ingramcontent.com/pod-product-compliance
Lightning Source LLC
Chambersburg PA
CBHW030540180626
46810CB00005B/1945